LOOK AT ME

The Debut (A Start in Life)
Providence

LOOK AT ME

PANTHEON BOOKS

NEW YORK

ANITA BROOKNER

All rights reserved under International and Pan-American Copyright
Conventions. Published in the United States by Pantheon Books, a
division of Random House, Inc., New York. Originally published in
Great Britain by Jonathan Cape Ltd., London.

Library of Congress Cataloging in Publication Data

Brookner, Anita.
Look at me.

I. Title.
PR6052.R5875L6   1983   823'.914   82-18968
ISBN 0-394-52944-8

Manufactured in the United States of America
First American Edition

O N E

Once a thing is known it can never be unknown. It can only be forgotten. And, in a way that bends time, so long as it is remembered, it will indicate the future. It is wiser, in every circumstance, to forget, to cultivate the art of forgetting. To remember is to face the enemy. The truth lies in remembering.

My name is Frances Hinton and I do not like to be called Fanny. I work in the reference library of a medical research institute dedicated to the study of problems of human behaviour. I am in charge of pictorial material, an archive, said to be unparalleled anywhere else in the world, of photographs of works of art and popular prints depicting doctors and patients through the ages. It is an encyclopaedia of illness and death, for in early days few maladies were curable and they seem therefore to have exerted a dreadful fascination over the minds of men. We are particularly interested in dreams and madness, and our collection is rather naturally weighted towards the incalculable or the undiagnosed. Problems of human behaviour still continue to baffle us, but at least in the Library we have them properly filed.

I work with Olivia, my friend, and we send off for

photographs to museums and galleries, and when they arrive we mount them on sheets of cardboard and type all the relevant information about them on a paper slip which is then fixed to the mount. It is extremely interesting, in a hopeless sort of way. So many lunatics, so many punitive hospitals, so much deterioration. And so much continuity, so much still unsolved. That, I am glad to say, is not my job, although it seems to exercise the minds of most of the people for whom I work.

Take the problem of melancholy, for example. I could almost write a treatise on melancholy, simply from looking through the files. In old prints melancholy is usually portrayed as a woman, dishevelled, deranged, surrounded by broken pitchers, leaning casks, torn books. She may be sunk in unpeaceful sleep, heavy limbed, overpowered by her inability to take the world's measure, her compass and book laid aside. She is very frightening, but the person she frightens most is herself. She is her own disease. Dürer shows her wearing a large ungainly dress, winged, a garland in her tangled hair. She has a fierce frown and so great is her disarray that she is closed in by emblems of study, duty, and suffering: a bell, an hourglass, a pair of scales, a globe, a compass, a ladder, nails. Sometimes this woman is shown surrounded by encroaching weeds, a cobweb undisturbed above her head. Sometimes she gazes out of the window at a full moon, for she is moonstruck. And should melancholy strike a man it will be because he is suffering from romantic love: he will lean his padded satin arm on a velvet cushion and gaze skywards under the nodding plume of his hat, or he will grasp a thorn or a nettle and indicate that he does not sleep. These men seem to me to be striking a bit of a pose, unlike the women, whose melancholy is less picturesque. The women look as if they are in the grip of an affliction too serious to be put into words. The men, on the other hand, appear to have dressed up for the occasion, and are anxious to put a noble face on their suffering. Which shows that nothing much has changed since the sixteenth century, at least in that respect.

Cures for melancholy include music and scourging. It is thought that some of the great religious figures of the past were melancholics. El Greco even chose models from the asylum of Toledo for his pictures of saints and apostles.

Next to melancholy in our filing system is madness, and this section too is heavily patronized. Here, the good news is that quite a bit has changed: madmen were once thought to be incredibly amusing, and there are far too many popular prints, most of them English, I am sorry to say, of funny men hitting themselves on the head or pulling faces at one another. But of course this material can be very serious indeed, particularly as quite a few artists have a close understanding of this sad condition. How powerful lunatics are! Once they were nude, struggling, chained. They tore their hair and hid their faces. A medieval emblem of a madman, on a Tarot card, shows a giant figure dressed in skins, a raven on his shoulder, playing the bagpipes. Only Géricault seems to have shown the mad as creatures of dignity, but of course he lived in the great age when the shackles of the insane were struck off, and in some cases the patients were allowed to wear their own clothes. And it is said that Géricault was mad himself, at least from time to time, and this would undoubtedly deepen his sense of kinship with this strange population. The world of obsession, of delusion, turns the eyes of Géricault's madmen red with suspicion, or opens them wide with uncorrupted innocence. Sometimes they think they are children, or generals, or kings. In a horrendous picture by Goya, a large vaulted room with a high window is filled with a mêlée of furious nude figures, some fighting, some grovelling, some simply crawling on the ground, yet even among these barely human creatures some have adorned themselves with paper crowns or with feathers or with chains of office. Goya also shows a figure slipping away from the normal human condition, with an animal head and huge feet, his body electrified by a storm of black chalk strokes. I know very little about Goya's state of mind apart from the fact that it must have been unenviable. He seems to have been on the edge of the tolerable all his life.

We also have a full range of deaths, and here the fear is unending. Death too can be a woman, with a skull, misleadingly handsome. But death is usually a skeleton which one perceives to be male. Death can menace the mother with the child, can invade the comfortable dwelling of the merchant, can interrupt the miser counting his gold or the scholar in his study. Death can waylay the bridegroom and his bride; death can attend the wedding feast. Death, wearing a crown, his bony foot on a globe, holds a glass inscribed with the words, The mirror that flatters not. And death is unpeaceful, as I well know. At the end temptation comes in the form of gargoyles and devils, and a fight for the soul of the dying will be waged by angels around his bed of suffering.

The section most popular in our Library is the one devoted to dreams. There are dreams of women, dreams of God, dreams of whirlwinds, of giant birds, of dogs, of fame. St Helena dreams of the True Cross, which she was later to find. The most famous dream image of all shows a man with his head sunk on his folded arms and bats flying all around him. All these dreams seem terribly disturbing. I never dream myself, and I suppose I am very lucky. I am also fortunate enough to be in excellent health, and this fact, and the fact that I have no specialist knowledge, makes my work tolerable. If I were to be afflicted in any way, I doubt if I could look at this stuff all day. Fortunately, even for one as invulnerable as myself, there are images of good doctors, although it is true that too many of them seem to spend their time pulling teeth or burrowing into open wounds with large iron instruments or squinting at flasks of urine. But I try to remember that picture painted by Goya (you see how his name keeps coming up) as an act of friendship towards his own doctor, Dr Arrieta. I have a peculiar fondness for this image. It shows the painter in a dressing gown; he faces the spectator in an extremity of suffering, the structure of his face and body disintegrating beneath the gravity of his pain, his expression both naked and disbelieving. Behind him stands his doctor, a small man, neat, hopeful, resolute. He extends one arm round the shoulders of his patient, and with the other proffers a remedy. I believe that on that occasion Goya did not die, although he may not in fact have ever fully recovered. Nobody knows what the illness was, but it was clearly terrible. Dr Arrieta was something of an expert on the plague and he went to Africa to investigate it. Whether he ever caught it or not I do not know. My information runs out here.

Most of the real work in the Library is done by Dr Leventhal, the librarian, who combs the many reference books in search of maladies and images of maladies and who then passes the information on to Olivia or myself. We do the work of mounting and filing, of collecting offprints of learned articles, and we also look after the visitors who come to consult our archives. We are not very well known to the general public nor would we wish to be, but we cater for our own staff of doctors and for outside specialists and the odd, the very odd, visitor. At the moment we can count on Mrs Halloran and Dr Simek. Mrs Halloran is a wild-looking lady with a misleading air of authority who claims to be in touch with the other side and who is trying to prove her theory that the influence of Saturn is responsible for most anomalies of behaviour. You get a lot of borderline cases in libraries. Dr Simek is an extremely reticent Czech or Pole (we are not quite sure which and we do not see that it is our business to enquire). He is working, on a series of tiny file cards, on the history of the treatment of depressions, or melancholia, as it used to be known, and he comes in every day. They both come in every day, largely, I suspect, because the Library is so very well heated.

Mrs Halloran's attempts to engage Dr Simek in conversation – efforts which he courteously and wordlessly ignores – usually reach some sort of climax when they both want to study the same folder of photographs. Mrs Halloran always wins, because she makes such a noise that it is in everybody's interest to shut her up, just as some people get a lot of sympathy because they complain all the time. On these occasions Dr Simek smiles, inclines his head, and says, 'Miss Frances, if you would be so kind ...', and requests more photographs. I always deal with him because Olivia is more brutal and has been known to tell Mrs Halloran to keep quiet or go to another library. Mrs Halloran knows that she would not last five minutes outside the confines of this peculiar place, half study, half nursery, and subsides, for a time, at least. Round about midday she says, 'Either of you girls coming round to the Bricklayers?', and we say, as we always do, that we are so busy that we are simply going to have a quick sandwich in the canteen. Mrs Halloran goes out for a couple of hours and comes back breathing rather heavily, her concentration gone, as is proved by the way she gazes out of the window for long periods and taps on the table with one or other of her massive onyx rings. She does not seem to know that she is doing this, and eventually Dr Simek looks up, inclines his head politely, and says, 'Madam, if you would be so kind ...' I think this was the first phrase he learned when he came to this country. He never goes out to lunch. He never seems to eat at all. When I bring Olivia her tea I sometimes take him a cup, which is a bore because then Mrs Halloran wants one too, and then Dr Leventhal appears in the doorway that divides the Library from his office and wants to know if we are having a party, and could we please remember that silence is the rule. He is the sort of man who only breaks his own silence in order to utter a derogatory remark. But he is otherwise quite harmless. I would not say that we were genuinely fond of him (that would hardly be appropriate) but he is easy to work for, a mild, heavy man, probably shy, probably lonely, very correct, easily tolerated. We all get on very well.

The potential boredom of this routine is broken by the visits of one or other of the Institute's own doctors, particularly one of the two whose research we are funding, James Anstey or Nick Fraser. Particularly Nick Fraser. Nick is everybody's favourite, even Dr Leventhal's. For as long as Olivia and I have known him he has been distinguished by that grace and confidence of manner that ensure success. He is tall and fair, an athlete, a socialite, well-connected, good-looking, charming: everything you could wish for in a man. Our all-England hero, Olivia once called him, in those days when she was more than a little in love with him. She may still be, for all I know, but she never mentions it and I don't ask. Sometimes her mouth tightens after one of his lightning visits when, in a mood of general hilarity or euphoria, he sweeps in, flings his arms around Mrs Halloran ('Delia, you old monster, what are you doing here?'), demands, with an urgent clicking of the fingers, a whole pile of photographs, looks at his watch, remembers he has an appointment, begs me, with his ravishing smile, to take them up to his room, and sweeps out again, leaving a trail of disorder and excitement. Dr Leventhal appears in his doorway, sees who it is, and subsides. 'Don't take them,' says Olivia. 'Why should you?' 'Oh, but I must,' I reply. 'I can't hold up his work. He's so brilliant. I mean his work is.'

'You mean he is. You have succumbed, just like everybody else. The discreet charm of the bourgeoisie vanquished once more by the brutal fascination of the upper classes.'

She talks like that. She was brought up in a strictly socialist household. Also, she pines a little, I think, because Nick is married to the equally dazzling Alix, whom Olivia, for various reasons, can't stand. We have never discussed this because on some matters reticence is preferable, particularly when feelings are liable to change. We are both rather old-fashioned, I suppose, and although our friendship is deep and sincere, we do not really subscribe to the women's guerrilla movement. I think we like to maintain a certain loyalty to the men who have, or have had, our love and affection; we regard ourselves in some way as being concerned with their honour. Ridiculous, really, when you come to think of it. I have learned that there is no reciprocity in these matters. But in any case Olivia is a creature of such high breeding that she would consider such a discussion to be in questionable taste. So we never say anything, although I have seen her eyes darken and her face grow paler than usual after one of these visits. There is no hope, of course. I think she saw that even before I did. She is very brave.

So I struggle up the stairs with Nick's photographs and he leans back in his chair for an instant and smiles and says, 'Darling Fanny. *What* a good girl you are', and I go downstairs again, and do something strenuous and unpleasant, like a lot of very brisk filing, until Mrs Halloran comes back from her lunch and knocks something off one of the tables with her bag and the afternoon gets under way.

Nick is also working on depression and it sometimes surprises me that he talks to Mrs Halloran, whom he knows from the pub, rather than to Dr Simek, who was apparently quite an authority in his own country. I would have thought that they would have a great deal in common. Dr Simek has often tried to retain his attention but he is too courteous, too resigned, and Nick is always too much in demand for them ever to be able to get together. Dr Simek seems to accept this, as he accepts everything else: the un-European character of this Library, with its cups of tea and its ash-trays and Mrs Halloran, who is sometimes quite drunk, and the fact that one of the librarians is more or less immobile. I feel that it is just as well that Dr Simek is working largely on the nineteenth century for there is no doubt that Nick will sweep the board of honours when he publishes his own work on depression. Dr Simek always waits until Nick has finished his joke with Mrs Halloran, his head on one side, his lips slightly pursed, his eyes looking studiously down at the photograph in his slightly trembling hand, and when the laughter has died down, he clears his throat and says, 'Dr Fraser, if you would be so kind ...', which is his all-purpose phrase, and he shows him the photograph. Nick, who is always in a tearing hurry, and who has to combine his research with his professional duties and a full social life, makes a disappointed face. 'Joseph,' he says, 'it really is too ridiculous that we never have time to discuss this properly. Why don't you come to dinner one evening? I'll get my wife to give you a ring.'

'I have no telephone,' says Dr Simek, as might have been expected. 'Perhaps now we could ...'

'I'll get her to ring here,' Nick assures him. 'One of the girls will take a message.' Actually we are not allowed

13

to use the telephone, which is in Dr Leventhal's office and which is in fact his telephone, but I don't suppose he would mind as it has to do with research. I assume that they have had this dinner, which Dr Simek certainly looks as if he needs, but he shows no signs of leaving Nick alone, and Nick sometimes advances behind his back with exaggerated wariness, willing him not to turn round. Dr Simek never does turn round: I suppose that, being a foreigner, he does not recognize the informal approach. Of course he knows that Nick is in the room because he has seen him come in, and I think he also knows that Nick is avoiding him, but he merely purses his lips and gets on with his work. Curiously enough, Mrs Halloran and I find ourselves in some sort of complicity with Nick on these occasions. Our eyes follow his progress round the room, and he gives us both a grateful wink as he tiptoes out.

It is strange how this fails to annoy me, although as a rule I am sensitive to bad manners. It is just that occasionally, very occasionally, one meets someone who is so markedly a contrast with the general run of people that one's instinctive reaction is one of admiration, indulgence, and, no doubt, if one is not very careful indeed, of supplication. I am not arguing the rights and wrongs of this: I am simply stating the facts as they appear to me. And not only to me, for I have noticed that extremely handsome men and extremely beautiful women exercise a power over others which they themselves have no need, or indeed no time, to analyse. People like Nick attract admirers, adherents, followers. They also attract people like me: observers. One is never totally at ease with such people, for they are like sovereigns and one's duty is to divert them. Matters like worth or merit rarely receive much of their attention, for, with the power of choice which their looks bestow on them, they can change their minds whenever they care to do so. Because

14

of their great range of possibilities, their attention span is very limited. And their beauty has accustomed them to continuous gratification.

I find such people – and I have met one or two – quite fascinating. I find myself respecting them, as I would respect some natural phenomenon: a rainbow, a mountain, a sunset. I recognize that they might have no intrinsic merit, and yet I will find myself trying to please them, to attract their attention. 'Look at me,' I want to say. 'Look at me.' And I am also intrigued by their destinies, which could, or should, be marvellous. I will exert myself for such people, and I will miss them when they leave. I will always want to know about them, for I tend to be in love with their entire lives. That is a measure of the power that they exert. That is why I join Nick in a smile of complicity when he spares himself the boredom of a conversation with Dr Simek. It is a kind of law, I suppose.

'That', says Mrs Halloran heavily, after every other one of Nick's disruptive visits to the Library, 'is one hell of a man', at which point Olivia asks her to be quiet and observe the rule of silence, and Mrs Halloran says, 'Miss Benedict, why don't you get hold of that sodding offprint I've been asking for every day for the last month instead of telling me what to do? I don't tell you what to do, do I?'

'You just have,' says Olivia, who is never less than totally composed, and after that they subside for an hour or two, until dissension breaks out again over the matter of whether Mrs Halloran gets a cup of tea or not. Oddly enough, Olivia quite likes her, although I suspect that she finds her life in the Library rather painful at times. But she never says anything. How could she? Apart from her unspoken love for Nick, there is her unspoken dislike of his behaviour. Neither, of course, will ever register with him. It is when I think about this that I congratulate myself on not being in love with anyone. I am not in love with Nick. I am not in love with Dr Leventhal (difficult to imagine) or Dr Simek (even more difficult) or even with James Anstey, even though he is tall and ferocious-looking and presentable and not married and undoubtedly what Mrs Halloran would call a bit of a handful.

I used to make my mother laugh when I went home in the evenings and described the characters who came into the Library. 'My darling Fan,' she used to say, her eyes widening, 'I think you have a gift.' She knew all their habits, and where they lived; it was like a serial story to her. She encouraged me to write it all down, and so I bought the usual large exercise book and kept a sort of diary, and I like to think that one day I will use this material and write a comic novel, one of those droll and piquant chronicles enjoyed by dons at Oxford and Cambridge colleges. I could do it, I know. Since my mother died, I have had no one to talk to about these things, no one who is so interested, who knows the characters, who wants to find out what happens next, who responds with such delight. So I tend to write a bit more, these days, when I get home in the evenings, although it is not the same, and I have to struggle to keep a note of despondency out of what gets put down. In fact sometimes I have to struggle quite hard, because I do hate low-spirited people. I would even say I hate unfortunate people, which is why I do not enquire too closely about Dr Simek. I have put all that sort of thing behind me.

And it seems that I am right to do so, because a short story I wrote – actually about the Library, although heavily disguised, of course – was once published. I was not on the whole as pleased with it as everyone else seemed to be, but I'm glad that my mother knew about it before she died. It was one I hadn't read to her, which

16

in an odd way may have been just as well. She always took people more seriously than I try to do.

So the days go by in an orderly fashion. I get up, I come to work, I have lunch with Olivia, I stick on the photographs, I even try to work out some of the pictures for myself. I find the power of images very strong, even when I do not understand them. Sometimes an image stands for something that will only be understood in due course. It is a mnemonic, a cryptogram, very occasionally a token of precognition. I pay very great attention to images, both at the Library and away from it. I spend a lot of time on my own, and the contents of my mind, which is nothing out of the ordinary, amaze me with their random significance. That is why I like the Library, not only for the task of classification which is its main purpose, but for the potency of its images, like the Fool on the Tarot card, or Melancholia with her torn book, or Goya with his doctor.

The day goes on very peacefully, and eventually it gets dark and we start to tidy up. The light goes out in Dr Leventhal's office, and we ask Dr Simek which photographs he wants kept out for the following day. After a time he puts on his old tight foreign overcoat and his astrakhan hat, ties his grey muffler, smoothes his heavy brown gloves over those permanently shaking hands, bows slightly to both of us, and leaves. Mrs Halloran asks if either of us is coming round to the Feathers, which she patronizes in the evenings, and when we say that we are expected for dinner somewhere, she tugs a comb through her wiry hair, flings on her tweed cape, says, 'All right, be like that', and sweeps out of the room. She is a noisy woman. I once tried to find out why she came here; she does not really need our resources for those articles she writes in psychic magazines, but Olivia says that she lives in a private hotel in South Kensington and has to get out in the daytime, and besides, she hates

17

to be alone. And I imagine she gets paid more if she includes an illustration or two in her articles. She certainly stays here until the bitter end, and I have seen her face droop into a quite hopeless expression by the end of the day, the inside of her lower lip, which protrudes, looking empty and babyish.

I walk with Olivia to her car, and then I buy a newspaper and read it over a cup of coffee somewhere. I never want to go home and I put it off for as long as I can. I usually walk, from Manchester Square, where the Institute is situated, through to the Edgware Road and past all those horrible shops, full of corsets and nurses' uniforms and video cassettes and Indian food. I tramp past the launderettes and the cheap hairdressers with the mauve neon illuminations until I reach the more salubrious uplands. I always walk, whatever the weather. And when I have got rid of my restlessness and my tendency to brood, I let myself into the flat and I am in for the rest of the evening. I have something to eat and then I usually try to write. In that way I manage to get rid of the rest of the day.

I encounter resistance in myself, of course. That is only natural. I am quite young and I am aware that this is a dull life. Sometimes it seems like a physical effort simply to sit down at my desk and pull out the notebook. Sometimes I find myself heaving a sigh when I read through what I have already written. Sometimes the effort of putting pen to paper is so great that I literally feel a pain in my head, as if all the furniture of my mind were being rearranged, as if it were being lined up, being got ready for delivery from the storehouse. And yet when I start to write, all this heaviness vanishes, and I feel charged with a kind of electricity, not unpleasant in itself, but leading, inevitably, to greater restlessness.

Fortunately, I am not a hysterical person. I am used to being on my own and sometimes I doubt whether I could endure a lot of excitement. This remains an academic question, for I have never yet been tempted in this way. I am very orderly, and Spartan in my habits. I am famous for my control, which has seen me through many crises. By a supreme irony, my control is so great that these crises remain unknown to the rest of the world, and so I am thought to be unfeeling. And of course I never speak of them. That would be intolerable. If I ever suffer loneliness it is because I have settled for the harsh destiny of dealing with these matters by myself.

Sometimes I wish it were different. I wish I were beautiful and lazy and spoiled and not to be trusted. I wish, in short, that I had it easier. Sometimes I find myself lying awake in bed, after one of these silent evenings, wondering if this is to be my lot, if this solitude is to last for the rest of my days. Such thoughts sweep me to the edge of panic. For I want more, and I even think that I deserve it. I have something to offer. I am no beauty but I am quite pleasant-looking. In fact people tell me that I am 'attractive', which always depresses me. It is like being told that you are 'brilliant', which means precisely nothing. But apart from that, I am in good health and have ample private means. I have few bad habits, apart from my sharp tongue. I have no religion, but I observe certain rules of conduct with considerable piety. I feel quite deeply, I think. If I am not very careful, I shall grow into the most awful old battle-axe.

That is why I write, and why I have to. When I feel swamped in my solitude and hidden by it, physically obscured by it, rendered invisible, in fact, writing is my way of piping up. Of reminding people that I am here. And when I have ordered my characters, plundered my store of images, removed from them all the sadness that I might feel in myself, then I can switch on that current that allows me to write so easily, once I get started, and to make people laugh. That, it seems, is what they like to do. And if I manage this well enough and beguile all the dons and the critics, they will fail to register my real message, which is a simple one. If my looks and my manner were of greater assistance to me I could deliver this message in person. 'Look at me,' I would say. 'Look at me.' But since I am on my own in this matter, I must use subterfuge and guile, and with a bit of luck and good management this particular message will never be deciphered, and my reasons for delivering it in this manner remain obscure.

T W O

These odd feelings of isolation may have something to do with my immediate environment, which is, I suppose, anachronistic. Maida Vale is a very strange neighbourhood, I always think, full of huge blocks of flats which in their turn seem to be full of small elderly people. Very few of these people seem to be about in the streets, which are always deserted, and those who venture out for a spot of shopping wear enormous fur coats and have dogs and sticks. When I come home in the evenings I see no one, although I can smell enticing cooking smells behind the closed double doors on each landing. I imagine dinner parties being prepared; I imagine hostesses with silver hair and small diamond earrings leaning heavily forward to light candles on walnut tables. Their guests will probably have travelled no farther than next door or the floor below, but they will have dressed up for the occasion, the ladies in old but good black chiffon dresses, the gentlemen in velvet jackets and bow ties. They will all be in slight physical distress, appropriate to their age, but they will be very gallant and good-humoured, and they will exclaim in delight at the strength of the sherry in the consommé,

21

and compliment their hostess profusely. These excellent people attend lectures at the Victoria and Albert Museum and occasionally team up to go to the National Theatre, which they do not enjoy. 'My dear, I found it difficult to *breathe*,' they will say to each other. They usually make up a four for bridge, or sometimes two fours, and there will be a cup of tea for the ladies and a whisky and soda for the gentlemen at eleven-thirty. They will kiss each other affectionately as they leave, and insist, 'You must come to us next time.' I don't know any of these people, of course. I can simply smell their food, which is very good. Various ladies sent flowers when my mother died, but after I had written to thank them I threw away the cards. I am aware of a nod and a smile from behind a door, should it happen to be open when I pass, but as I am out all day, and as they apparently play bridge all night, or at least until eleven-thirty, there is hardly much chance for us to meet. Besides, they are all so much older than I am.

I am very much aware that this is a building for old people, with its red stair carpet and the heavy lift with the iron gates and the polished brass letter boxes and the small corpulent porter. The residents belong to that class and generation which was never told to lower its voice, so that cries of 'Phyllis! My dear!' ring out from floor to floor until the door shuts behind the fur-coated visitor. I have seen small grandchildren appear at Christmas, in coats with velvet collars; they are excessively well-behaved and hold their mother's hands. Their cheeks are quite flushed when they re-emerge, either from the Christmas cake so proudly produced ('Your great-grandmother's recipe, my darlings!') or at the prospect of opening the crackling parcels which they cradle in their arms. Things are even quieter in the summer. Then it is the turn of the old people to pay their children a visit, and from my window I hear the voices rise from the pavement and the sticks tap, and should I happen to look out I might see Mrs Hunt or Lady Cohen negotiating the difficult business of getting into the car. 'Goodbye, Mr Reardon, and thank you *so* much,' they cry as they rearrange their old legs in the narrow space. 'Goodbye, Madam,' says the porter, and he waits on the pavement until the car has moved safely on its way.

I am hardly aware of this place as home, although I have always lived here, and, as the flat now belongs to me there is no real reason for me to move, particularly as prices are so high at the moment. Indeed I am so excessively comfortable, and my life is so regulated, that the question only rarely crosses my mind. But that restlessness of which I spoke is in part caused by boredom and in part by lack of company. I sometimes have fantasies of a life in which I would spend evenings sitting on somebody's bed, exchanging confidences, keeping up with each other's love affairs, comparing clothes, trying out new hairstyles ... Although all that is hardly to my taste. But it is very difficult to invite anyone here. If life were suddenly to change and I were to make a completely new circle of friends I should have to do some radical rearranging. I am hardly likely to give dinner parties for ten or soirées for fifty people, although the rooms are big enough. And I can see that I should have a hard time disowning the furniture, of which I have grown inexplicably fond, although I spent some of my most critical years grumbling about it. The wind of change would have to blow very hard indeed for me to feel that I had at last taken possession of this place and was entitled to make it my own.

For in my mind it still belongs to my parents. My mother and father moved here during the war, when my father's job necessitated their being in London. They moved in very quickly, as one did in those days; within

23

a week they had got rid of their house in Surrey, which my mother was finding too difficult to manage. They took over the flat lock, stock and barrel as the owner was anxious to sell before she went to join her sister in America. That is how they came to inherit this extremely peculiar décor, which looks like something sprung direct from the brain of an ambitious provincial tart. Times being what they were, my parents did nothing to change it; they were in any case too wrapped up in each other, too fearful for the safety of each other, to care for their surroundings, so long as these were safe, warm, comfortable, and could keep danger at bay. Even when life settled down and became more normal than they ever dared to hope, they changed nothing, perhaps out of superstition. That is how I came to grow up with all manner of terrible cut-glass mirrors with bevelled edges hanging from chains over tiled fireplaces, shaggy off-white fitted carpets, zig-zag patterned rugs, nests of walnut tables, semicircular armchairs upholstered in pale creaking hide, standard lamps with polygonal ivory satin shades, white wrought-iron trellises over the radiators, a dining table massive enough to overshadow the ten dining room chairs whose seats are composed of beige brocade secured with brass studs, divan beds with headboards which sweep round to accommodate bedside cabinets, dressing tables with sheets of glass covering the surfaces and triple mirrors, and, *pièce de résistance*, a collection of china and glass birds, some rather large, which march along the shelves of highly polished pale wood bookcases with sliding doors made of yet more glass.

My mother domesticated this interior by inserting her many photographs of my father, and later of myself, under the topmost surface of her dressing table. She did not much care for her surroundings but she liked the solidity of the flat, which is in a reassuring stone building

24

on top of the Westminster Bank on the corner of Maida Vale and one of those quiet streets which go off in the direction of St John's Wood. A whining lift, with polished brass fittings, is presided over by the porter, Mr Reardon, who otherwise lives in a cubby-hole on the ground floor. My mother grew to love the solemn clash of the lift gates, for she felt protected and enclosed by them, and this was a need which grew in her with the years.

The flat is very large, much too large for me. In my parents' day this problem was solved by their finding Nancy, quite by accident. Nancy is from Ireland and they found her crying in a doorway after an air-raid which had flattened the house in which she had a room. They brought her home; she became their devoted maid and she has been here ever since. As these flats were built to accommodate servants, she has her own room and bathroom beyond the kitchen, which is large enough to serve as a sitting room for her. She is now pretty old and she will undoubtedly live here until she dies. She gets up very early and goes to Mass every day. She comes back and has her breakfast, by which time I have already gone to work. She goes out later to do the shopping and then she is in until the following morning. Her routine never varies. Every evening she used to serve my parents' dinner, so that my mother never had to do a lot, which was just as well, for her heart was weak and the doctor had warned her not to lift or carry anything. After my father's death, by which time my mother was so much more frail, Nancy would prepare her evening meal and give it to her on a tray. It came to be the same meal every evening: a cup of soup, a little chicken, some stewed fruit, all in tiny portions. As my mother grew weaker, the meal got smaller and more bland: the soup, which my mother barely touched, a few buttered crackers, a dish of custard or semolina.

Nowadays, if I am in, she serves the same meal to me, and however much I dislike it, I know that I cannot stop her doing this. 'Madam always liked it this way', she says, and her small but surprisingly flower-like blue eyes look at me in reproach and disappointment.

I have never known anyone grieve and mourn like Nancy. After my mother's death I was dry-eyed and stony-faced, glad that the ordeal was over. As I moved stiffly about the bedroom, opening curtains, sweeping all the useless pills into a plastic bag, stripping that terrible bed, Nancy sat in my mother's chair, like a frightened child, small tears creeping down her cheeks, wisps of grey hair sticking to her wet face. She thought me ruthless and snatched up my mother's slippers, just as I was about to throw them away, holding them to her, cradling them ... She had been fearless in her nursing. She would hold my mother's head, during those spasms of which I cannot bear to think, while I would fly in terror to the door. She would settle her for the night, smoothing her forehead on the pillow, taking her hand and patting it on the sheet. Or she would hold that hand and stroke it, the hand that had become so thin that the rings were stuck on with sellotape. But it was for me that my mother stayed awake, for my goodnight kiss, which I came to dread, like all the rest. 'My darling Fan', she would murmur, and Nancy would stay with her until she fell asleep.

Like my mother, I have changed nothing in the flat. Although the days are so different, the nights, when I hear Nancy shuffling down the corridor to lock up, and shuffling back again, are just the same. The food is the same. And I can make no more impression on the décor than did my mother. Nancy becomes distressed when I suggest that she remove those china and glass birds which she dusts every day and washes once a week. The flat is much too big, but we have shut off the extra three

26

bedrooms and we do not get in each other's way. Besides, I can walk to the office from here. Sometimes it seems impossible and I dream of a candid attic somewhere, all white and empty, looking over trees. Then I finger the gold brocade curtains, with their tasselled gold tie-backs, and I think how my mother used to stand at the window, waiting for my father to come home. And then I know that I will stay.

Once Nick and Alix brought me home, when I first knew them. They looked around in amazement and I thought appreciation, for it is very comfortable. But when they saw the birds, recently washed by Nancy, they caught each other's eye and within seconds they were helpless with laughter, staggering, leaning in pain over the backs of the awful hide chairs. They would sober up, only to start off again, and I had to join in, although I felt ... What did I feel? That I had not really looked at them before, had not noticed how absurd they were. I put them into a drawer when Nick and Alix had left, but Nancy took them out again the following morning and gave them an extra wash. I said nothing.

Otherwise Alix seemed very keen on the flat, although she gave way to another paroxysm when she asked for an ash-tray and was given one in green malachite with a green malachite cockatoo on the rim, gazing down as if into a tropical lagoon. As I don't smoke myself I had never really noticed it, but I did manage to relegate it to the back of a cupboard after they had gone. Nancy found it, of course, and it was soon back in its old place.

Alix and Nick, unexpected, unhoped for visitors, bringing me home in the car after I had had dinner with them, and invited in with a mixture of eagerness and panic. They, mildly curious, always willing to be diverted, consented to sit down but not to remove coats, scarves, gloves. It was not a real visit at all. They would not let me pour them a drink or make more coffee, and

27

yet they lingered, frankly taking an inventory. 'I'm interested in people's houses,' said Alix. 'I used to have a very beautiful one of my own.' At which she heaved a sigh, and pulled out her cigarettes and her lighter. 'Don't, darling,' Nick commiserated, but at that moment I tendered the cockatoo ash-tray and provided a timely diversion. We all joined in her laughter, grateful to her for having raised her spirits again. I saw, even then, that Nick was perpetually on the watch for a change in her mood, and I thought how fortunate she was.

Pulling herself together with an effort which made her seem more authoritative than usual, Alix said it was ridiculous my having all this space, and that I should put Nancy into a home and take their spare room, which they were always thinking of letting in order to bring in some extra money. She said they could keep an eye on me that way, and I am thinking about it, although Nancy is a problem, and I have said nothing to her yet. Alix became quite excited when she saw the large bathroom with its pale green thirties' tiles and the bath which is so much bigger than theirs. Indeed, the whole flat is more their size than mine, as Alix said, and became impatient when I said that I preferred theirs. 'You don't know what it's like to live there,' she said bitterly. 'And anyway you've only seen it once.' Nick always gets unhappy when she starts on about their flat, and said, 'Darling, why don't you ask Fanny to sell you her flat, then she could take ours. It's more her size.' This form of indirect speech struck me as odd; basically there was no reason why he could not have put this question himself. But of course he doesn't really want to move; he just wants to make her happy. Her eyes narrowed, as they always do when mention is made of either buying or selling. She does mind it so dreadfully that she has come down in the world, as she says, pulling a comically tragic face, and that her family's estate in Jamaica has been sold to pay debts. When money is mentioned she draws her fur coat around her and shivers, for she remembers how she never spent a winter in England until she learned the facts of her father's insolvency. One must never mention either money or the cold to Alix. It makes Nick too wretched, as well as Alix herself.

So we live in this flat, Nancy and I, and we hardly ever speak. Of course, I am not here in the daytime, and now, thank God, hardly ever here in the evenings either. There is no point in changing anything. There is more than enough money, I am almost ashamed to say, thinking of poor Alix shivering in her fur coat, although it is not the sort of money that Alix would be inclined to respect. My father originally inherited a toy factory in the East End from his rather idiosyncratic family. He sold it as soon as he could, and with his friend Sydney Goldsmith formed a sort of partnership for investing on the Stock Market. They were absurdly successful. They turned themselves into a limited company, had lunch two or three times a week in order to discuss business, diversified, and ended up rather rich. That is where my money comes from, and I care for it as little as my father did. He was mainly concerned with earning a living in a way which would leave him entirely free to devote himself to my mother. I think Sydney was the brains of the partnership. He was very fond of my father, and their friendship seems to have had a peaceful sweetness about it that I have never encountered since. Indeed, all the emotions of those days remain unmatched ... After my father's death Sydney would visit my mother once a month, always with a box of chocolates, which she gave to Nancy after he had left. 'Well, Fanny,' he would say to me in the hall, divesting himself of his sharp camel hair coat and his soft brown trilby hat (he always dressed like a gangster), 'how is our dear one today?' And he would sit with my mother and talk to her of my father,

29

although I think he loved her himself. Their innocence, it seems to me now, was unbounded. I slightly dreaded these visits, which followed the same pattern, the same antique pattern. I always had to stay in for Sydney's visits, and although I recognized that he was, as my father claimed, the dearest of men, I would count the minutes until he took his leave. This too followed a prescribed pattern. He would bend over my mother's chair and kiss her forehead and say, 'Any time, Beatrice. Call on me any time. My time is yours.' He would always have a word with Nancy on the way out, would in fact make a point of knocking on the kitchen door to thank her for tea. She loved him too. He still comes, although I am rarely here. I believe he lives in Worthing now. I think he said something about moving down there. Cutting adrift, he said.

The men in my mother's life were like priests, ministering to her. They loved her in a way I hope I am never loved, my father, Sydney Goldsmith, and Dr Constantine, who looked after her for so many years. It is why I seek the company of the young, the urbane, the polished, the ambitious, the prodigiously gifted, like Nick and his friends. In my mother's world, at least in those latter days, the men were kind, shy, easily damaged, too sensitive to her hurts. I never want to meet such men again. In a way I prefer them to be impervious, even if it means that they are impervious to me. I can no longer endure the lost look in the eye, the composure too easily shattered, the waning hope. I now require people to be viable, durable. I try to catch hold of their invulnerability and to apply it to myself. I want to feel that the world is hard enough to withstand knocks, as well as to inflict them. I want evidence of good health and good luck and the people who enjoy both. Those priestly ministrations, that simple childish cheerfulness, that delicacy of intention, that sigh immediately suppressed, that welcoming of routine attentions, that reliance on old patterns, that fidelity, that constancy, and the terror behind all of these things ... No more.

There is absolutely no need for me ever again to pretend that everything is all right. It is not, nor was it ever. It was unendurable, and I trained myself to endure it. The sad and patient virtues that seem to be enshrined in the very fabric, the very furnishings of this flat – the flightiness of its details battling unsuccessfully against the gravity of its overall demeanour – none of this has any further part to play in my existence. The blamelessness that flourished within these walls left us all deficient in vices with which to withstand the world, deficient in the sort of knowledge that protects and patronizes one's ventures. I know now that one needs to be as cunning as Ulysses in order to negotiate one's own passage. I believe that I have learned this lesson – I certainly hope that I have – and I intend to put my knowledge to good use, although I am not sure how. If necessary I shall write myself into a new way of life, and it will be a very amusing one. I have a long way to go, that I know. The old pattern still flourishes, because it was so complete, because everything here conspires to prolong it. It is like a long old age, forever forlorn and waiting for the end. Every morning now I hurry to get up and out of the flat, before Nancy gets back from Mass; I hurry to the Library, ready to observe the endless foolishness of serious preoccupation. I note every quirk of the behaviour around me, and when I get home I write it all down and I feel the weight of all that virtue lift, leaving me lighter and almost ready to begin again.

I shall probably stay here until Nancy dies, or leaves, which is improbable, although she has a sister in Cork. It is her home as much as it is mine, for I am ready to leave and have been for some time. I should like to move nearer to Nick and Alix, if not actually into their flat. I

31

need their high spirits, their energy, their durability. I need to participate in the life that they seem to generate; I need those impromptu meals, those last minute decisions, that ease. Here all is cautious, prudent, safe. The lift gates clash, and Nancy shuffles on her worn slippers, and sometimes that tray appears in front of me with the same tiny meal prepared and I shudder inwardly, although I eat it to please her. I could never hurt her. But she appears to think that nothing has changed, and that it never will, and she doesn't realize (why should she?) that this frightens me.

It is all so different at the Frasers'. Alix, who has had servants all her life, can't cook a thing except steak and spaghetti, which in fact she does rather well, so that her spaghetti has become 'her' spaghetti, and people congratulate her on it. She has this amusing way of interrogating absolute strangers if she thinks that they look interesting, and we have often gone down to the restaurant in the evening, just the three of us, and ended up with two more people, or three, or often just one, for she is always fascinated by people who are on their own; I don't suppose she knows many. Everyone succumbs to Alix, who can ask the most outrageous questions without giving offence, and after a time they find they want to confide in her, and they usually do. They ring her up, usually the morning after they have met, and I am sure they all feel that they have made a significant acquaintance. I think they wait, as I did, for that first invitation. 'You must come and have some of my spaghetti,' said Alix that day when she dropped into the Library after having lunch with Nick. 'It won't be much,' she added, 'because I've come down in the world', and she pulled a funny little face and looked at Nick, and he looked back, in a way that made me feel a little awkward, and they went off together and were away for quite a time. That is how and when I met her, although of course I have known Nick for much longer. He is always in and out of the Library.

Anyway, I went round to dinner one evening, the very day after I had met Alix, and I was enchanted. I loved everything: the little flat off the King's Road, and the tiny kitchen where I watched her cook the famous spaghetti, which was very good, and the spare room where I left my coat, and which is actually rather small ... Above all I loved the feeling of being taken over by Alix, by somebody with her strength and her decisiveness, after that kingdom of the shades in which I had been living for so long. We had quite a bit of time together before Nick came in, and she told me all about her marvellous childhood in Jamaica, or travelling about the world with her father, and how she misses all that vivid and strenuous life. I suppose it is rather dull being a doctor's wife in London after all that, but the amazing thing is that she really takes an interest in Nick's work and is always willing to help. I think that is marvellous of her, spending so much of her time with people who are unfit or depressed, and cheering them up. I can't think of any greater tonic than talking to Alix. I know that people think the world of her and I could see how she must invigorate them; it is a gift she has. She was telling me of her success with one particularly unfortunate man, and how everyone had been impressed. She said that she thought it was because she was the sort of woman who understood his problems, but added, with a sigh, that it was all very trying and distressing, and not what she was used to.

I said that I thought she was performing a great service.

She sighed again. 'One likes to think so,' she said. 'And if it helps Nick ... After all, that's my job now. And of course I am totally trustworthy. Everyone knows that. I am a *mine* of secrets.'

Again I expressed appreciation.

'And what about you?' she asked. 'What do you do apart from drudge in that ridiculous library?' I told her what a help it had been to work on so steadily after my mother's death, when I realized that it was my only protection, how the structure of the working day, the very banality of it, had helped me to compose myself after that wearying and bewildering time, how the silent presence of Dr Leventhal and Olivia had provided fixed points in the dizzying perspective of my new solitude . . .

'Oh, you're an orphan,' she cried, with comic emphasis. 'Darling,' she cried to Nick who had come through the door at that moment, 'she's an orphan! Little Orphan Fanny!' She made it sound as if it should be in capital letters. She made it sound funny and silly, and I felt better about it, and they have called me Fanny or Little Orphan Fanny ever since.

After that we didn't talk any more because Nick had brought home a man with whom he had been arm wrestling in the pub, and this man, who was Irish, told us his entire life story, and it was really very interesting.

I worried about asking them back, although at that stage I drew the line at the Irishman, because I knew somehow that Nancy would resent it. She doesn't cook much now and as we have practically never had visitors in the evening she likes to lock up early and any alteration to her routine upsets her and makes her fearful. I explained this to Alix, and as it turned out I needn't have worried because they usually eat out. There is a restaurant on the ground floor of their block of flats, and they find it much more convenient to eat there. This was delightful news to me because it meant that I could join them without feeling guilty about it, and pay my way or treat them at the same time.

I went there with them the following week and that

34

was another revelation. As an eating place it has the advantage of convenience, but the whole point is that this is where Alix meets her friends. She is one of those fortunate women who create circles of loyal friends wherever she goes, so that being with her is like belonging to a club. She is particularly friendly with a terrifically aristocratic Italian lady called Maria, who lives in one of the flats, and who has had an equally fascinating life. Maria and Alix are such friends that they can say terrible things to each other and call each other all sorts of names and still end up roaring with laughter. Maria is very handsome in that high-boned haughty way you sometimes find in North Italian women; I say handsome rather than beautiful because she is tall and very commanding. She has the same easy manner as Alix and is on excellent terms with all the other diners. I got the impression that all the regulars eat early and all Alix's friends come later, so that an evening spent in the company of Alix and Maria, and Nick, of course, is an evening unlike any other.

I was dazzled, delighted. We spent a whole evening there, Maria sitting at our table and smoking, and it was all the Bohemian evenings I had ever read about. Maria is apparently rather rich, although her financial affairs are quite spectacularly complicated on account of her divorce: she and Alix devote much of their time to this problem. She prefers to stay on in London, I gathered, where she has many friends. Many of them seemed to trickle in that evening and she greeted them with great enthusiasm, moving from one table to another, or lobbing shouts of recognition as people came through the door. Some of them made mock dodging motions as they came in, but they didn't get past Maria, whom Nick described as Italy's very own nuclear warhead. 'We're all terrified of her,' he added. 'If we're not careful she'll see that we don't get any dinner. She can't bear bores.'

Maria cuffed him round the head and he made as if to hit her back and then she really hit him and he shouted 'Unfair!' and they both collapsed with laughter.

'This is Fanny,' said Alix, with a ceremonious clearing of her throat. 'Be nice to her. She's an orphan.'

'Hello, Fanny,' said Maria, offering a large hand, which I shook. 'Welcome to the club.' I was so touched. All I managed to say was, 'Thank you.'

I tried to work it all out in my diary that evening when I was in bed. I felt as if I had been reprieved from the most dreadful emptiness. I had tried so hard to live sensibly and without undue expectation – for my expectations, alas, have often led me to make mistakes – and now that something so encompassing and vivifying had turned up I found it difficult to believe in my luck. Good things could only follow. I lay awake for a long time, and after some thought I decided to consider all the mistakes and the misconceptions of other days as water under the bridge. I had always desired to get matters right, and now it seemed as if I were to have just the help I needed. Some friends change your life, and although you know that they exist somewhere you do not always meet them at the right time. But now the road ahead seemed easier. I had been rescued from my solitude; I had been given another chance; and I had high hopes of a future that would cancel out the past.

T H R E E

The first time that I saw Nick and Alix together, I felt as if I were witnessing the vindication of nineteenth-century theories of natural selection. In the persons of Nick and Alix, the fittest had very clearly survived, leaving people like Olivia and me and Mrs Halloran and Dr Simek and Dr Leventhal to founder into unreproductive obscurity. So stunning was their physical presence, one might almost say their physical triumph, that I immediately felt weak and pale, not so much decadent as undernourished, unfed by life's more potent forces, condemned to dark rooms, and tiny meals, and an obscure creeping existence which would be appropriate to my enfeebled status and which would allow me gently to decline into extinction.

I had been used, of course, to Nick's hectic charm, his immense height, his generally golden quality. I had only to watch Olivia, and Mrs Halloran, for that matter, to see that his effect on women measured something very high on the Richter scale. How can I describe it? There was nothing particularly recondite about his careless endearments, which we had all grown used to; somehow, though, he managed to make one feel as if those

'Darlings' (Darling Fanny, Darling Olivia, Darling Delia) might one day be invested with significance. He seemed to prepare an atmosphere of affection for himself, yet I think we all felt that this was his natural climate. He was born to it; he was, or seemed to be, totally ignorant of the sad compromises and makeshifts, the substitutions and the fantasies, that constitute the emotional baggage of the average person.

We assumed that this diapason of love had followed him from home, that it had always been his natural element, that he had never lacked for it. If he used endearments it was because he had always heard them used towards himself. He struck one as a much-loved creature. Yet there was that restlessness, that urgency about him that reminded one, or perhaps brought to mind, made one conscious of, his undoubtedly intense sexuality. It was this particular dimension of his personality that made him so impressive. However spectacular and satisfying his life may have been in this respect, he always made one feel that he had the capacity for more, for other experience, for infinite fulfilment. He was a hunter. The combination of his golden and indiscriminate affection and his hard if random gaze at the women around him made one feel that possibly, and potentially, he might favour one. And it would have been a favour, of that there was no doubt. He was devoid of that element of need that makes some men, and rather a lot of women, unattractive in their desires; he was, in fact, desire in its pure state, but desire which was not necessarily active, desire which might awaken at unforeseen moments, in anyone's company, a random impulse, a natural condition.

We loved him as a phenomenon, a model of how ideal a man might be. And men loved him too, and oddly enough, they loved him for the same reason. They wished to be that model, to have that hard random glance, that assurance of easy victory. They would even have applauded, or at least condoned, any actual infidelity or indiscretion on his part. But he never was unfaithful or indiscreet, from what I gather. He was, rather, the possibility, I might even say the promise, of these things. He intimated that lawlessness would not trouble him, that his will would be served. He reminded one of the unfairness of life, and excited one with the idea that one might, if he wished, become a part of that unfairness, always reserved for the beautiful, the strong, the imperious, the healthy, the decisive, leaving the meek to inherit the earth or rather to live on the promise of that inheritance. Nick, or his appearance, convinced one that unfairness is built into every system, that the Prodigal Son, despite his deplorable behaviour and his unedifying record, was embraced by his father simply because he had come back, because there had been such vacancy while he was away.

We all felt rather like that about Nick. His impromptu appearances, always hasty, always unfinished, made us aware of the dullness that had preceded them. When he left the Library, we cleared up his untidiness, we carried his piles of photographs upstairs to his room, we never reminded him of the way he was always overdue with his returns, some of which were needed by other readers; we took messages for him, and made excuses for him, and refused, ever, to criticize him. We felt that he was a protected species, an example of the very highest breed of human being. So intense was this aura around him that one did not immediately connect it with the privileges he had undoubtedly enjoyed since birth. His parents, his home, his looks, his prowess, his school and university and professional records were all impeccable, yet we never thought that these things were causes. Rather, they were effects, which assured him confidence, but which were not directly responsible for that confidence. The fact that he always wore the right clothes, that he always went to the right barber, that he played the right games, these seemed to us to be explained by his munificent personality rather than by an enlightened use of the right instructions given from the very outset. We felt he was a natural leader of men. Yet his greatest gift to us was that intermittent speculative gaze, as if he might call one of us, from our dull safe places, to join him for an instant. He never did, of course. But the possibility, each of us thought, was there. Each of us – and every woman he had ever met, except Olivia – was just as actively waiting.

When I first saw him with Alix, I understood that we had been waiting in vain. I understood that he was, quite simply, unattainable. Unattainable, that is, by the likes of anyone who was not Alix or her equivalent. Alix was the only sort of woman whom Nick's sort of man would have chosen, and we were left with the distinct impression that there was only one example in each category: Nick and Alix. We were also left with the impression that they themselves knew and recognized this fact. It was when I saw them together, for the very first time, rejoicing in their complicity, their physical similarity, that I stopped any feeling I might have had towards Nick, other than the one I have already described. Instead, I fell in love with them both. Everybody did. They were used to it.

The first impression that one received was of a supreme married couple, matched in every way. The most obvious match was physical. They had a look of health and of exigence: one felt that no distant country would intimidate them, no contingency give them anxiety, no moment dare remain unfulfilled. One felt that the world was theirs, the physical world, that is, because it had been created for their diversion, and that if they wanted to feel the heat of the sun then they would quite naturally take off for Africa, rather than shiver and complain and wait for summer like the rest of us. 'I am interested in absolutely everything', I was to get used to Alix saying, and I did not question her, for with the entire universe open to her inspection, how could she not be? Whereas I tended to think in terms of the most obvious points of reference – neighbours, friends, colleagues, people in the bus queue – Alix and Nick would compare races, cultures, ethnic prototypes. What impressed me most about this was not only their breadth of view, but the fact that their lives contained no element of routine, that they would obey any summons, providing, of course, that it amused them to do so, answer any invitation, go anywhere, do anything. I thought them brave. They merely thought themselves sensible.

As they came through the door, that first afternoon, they appeared to walk with the same confident unhurried stride, and to look at each other rather than at their surroundings, as if the surroundings could wait, and were not, in any case, important enough to claim their attention. 'Pictured here enjoying a joke', as the captions said in those old copies of the *Tatler* that my mother used to pass on to Nancy and which are no doubt still in the kitchen cupboard somewhere. The Frasers' joke was of the same elevated and exclusive variety. It was no mere affair of hilarity, no spasm of passing amusement; it was, rather, an area of collusion, a shared knowledge of some ultimate delight which they desired to keep to themselves. One could easily imagine them strolling with the same unconcern, the same gaze directed towards each other rather than around them, through every circumstance of life; one could imagine them transplanted to the remotest civilization, the most exotic and untested of climates, and they would still consider themselves to be of primary and immediate importance.

I exaggerate, of course. Had I reflected for a single

41

moment, on the occasion of that first meeting, I would have told myself that there is no such thing as a charmed life, although appearances may lead one to suppose that this phenomenon exists. And I have always been susceptible to such appearances. Once I followed a girl in the street simply because she looked so lucky that I could not tear myself away from her. Apart from her youth and her beauty, she had the sort of assurance that promised well for her, as if her expectations were so high, so naturally high, that she had set a standard for herself that others would be encouraged to reach. She seemed to await the best of everything, and I remember staring at her as if she had descended from another planet. Being an observer in these matters does not always help one. Sometimes the scenes and people one observes impart their own message of exclusion. And yet the fascination of the rare perfect example persists, and it demands that one lay down one's pen and stalk it, study it, dissect it, learn it, love it. That was how I felt when I first saw Alix with Nick. I knew that I could never learn enough about them, but also that I might never understand what I learned. Therefore I watched them with particular care.

After that first impression of royal expectation, of perfect balance of forces, of mutual satisfaction, came a second impression, equally strong, and, to me, much more persuasive. At some level of my consciousness I recognized that they were impervious, that one could not damage them, that they would not founder through shock or deteriorate through neglect. They could not be hurt, except possibly by each other, and they were so clearly in accord that there was no division between them and thus no likelihood of a wound being inflicted. They were allies, partners, accomplices, moving at the same speed, liking and disliking the same things, possessing the same reserves. One could, if one wanted to, treat them roughly (though this was inconceivable); one would, in turn, want to be treated gently, for their greater strength was never in any doubt. The only danger to be feared from them was that they might find one insufficiently amusing, that they might be bored, that they might pass one over. It occurred to me that children might feel this way about superior parents, although I had never had such feelings about my own who were modest gentle people, greatly concerned for each other's tranquillity. With my sharp tongue I had had to be very careful not to hurt them, and they, of course, had never hurt me. But I had never had to try hard to please or divert or entertain them, either, and I think I longed to use my sharp tongue and to be restless and critical and amusing, even if it was at other people's expense. To me in those days it seemed like freedom not to have to care for anybody's feelings if I didn't want to. I hated every reminder that the world was old and shaky, that human beings were vulnerable, that everyone was, more or less, dying. I had lived with all this for far too long.

I needed to know that not everyone carries a wound and that this wound bleeds intermittently throughout life. I needed to be taught that life can put on a good turn of speed and bowl one along with it. I needed to learn, from experts, that pure egotism that had always escaped me, for the little I had managed to build up, and which had so far only gone into my writing, was quickly vanquished by the sight of that tremulousness, that lost look in the eye, that *disappointment* that seemed to haunt me, to get in my way, even to obtrude on my consciousness, when I was busy building up my resources of selfishness. I had only to see the dry, dyed hairs thickening in Mrs Halloran's comb as she prepared herself for her evening visit to the Feathers, or Dr Simek buttoning his old-fashioned gloves at the wrist, or to remember Nancy's stern but trusting blue eyes looking up at me, for the whole edifice to crumble. And this process would go on, despite my injunction to myself to ignore it. It would erupt in the form of images, which is appropriate, I suppose, since I deal with them all day, but they would irritate me as much as something obscuring my natural field of vision would irritate me. These tiny fugues are extremely random and unpredictable; they swim up from some area which I cannot control and which I should dearly love to forget about. Sometimes I see, sometimes I hear, forgotten episodes from my real life, and I always try very hard to invent a new life for myself so that I can get away from the old one, although to all intents and purposes that old life, which I had hitherto lived precariously and with a resignation mixed with impatience, had been very easy. It had been so easy that I was not satisfied with it. I suppose that is why I write, in order to recompose events, to make them sharper, funnier, than they really were. Above all, funnier. I write to be hard. I do not intend to spare any feelings, except, of course, my own.

It was, therefore, to my very great annoyance, that on the morning of the day of my first meeting with Alix Fraser, the day of that royal progress through life, that easy relegation of phenomena not found attractive, that I was haunted by the spectre of Dr Constantine. Dr Constantine was my mother's doctor, a small leathery man with a face like a nut and bandy legs. He looked more like a jockey than a doctor, and his strong Dublin accent reinforced this impression. I doubt if anyone took him seriously as a doctor; he was too shy, too full of awkward jokes, some of which were inaudible, to impress one with his superior knowledge. He could do very little for my mother except keep up her spirits, which he did by calling to see her every Saturday of her life. This was a visit which went according to a prescribed pattern. He would stay for exactly three-quarters of an hour, nursing a glass of whisky, which my mother would nod at me to pour out, and tell her all about the affairs of the neighbourhood. Small matters: the young man they were thinking of taking on as a partner, his receptionist's daughter's new baby. That sort of thing. He would take her pulse as he spoke and wind up by saying, 'Ah, you're doing fine.' She would say, 'Thanks to you, doctor', and he would blush, and my mother would add, 'And to my darling here.' Nancy and I would wait for him at the door and he would say again, 'She's doing fine', but he would never meet my eye. And one day ... One day I was summoned home by Nancy, who telephoned the Library, and when I got there it was to find my mother having an attack and Dr Constantine crouched over the telephone in the hall, his face red, his composure gone. 'I'm begging you, Matron,' he was saying. 'Find me a bed. Ah God, Matron, I can't deal with it here.' He was despairing, distraught, his small brown eye searching, somewhere beyond my head, for succour. Yet he dealt with it, because there was no bed free in the hospital, and in the end she died at home, and he was not there, and he apologized to me. He would have wept if I had not been very polite and formal and kept it short, that apology. I felt nothing. In any event, I felt less than he did.

He was not there. But I was.

So that on the morning of the day that Alix came to the Library it was extremely annoying to have vividly in my mind's eye the image of Dr Constantine crouched over the telephone, his face red, his small eye vacant and despairing, and to have in my mind's ear the sound of his voice. Begging. Without resource.

Also, and for no reason that I can identify, I saw a cigarette box that belonged to my father, made of rose-wood, with a marquetry inlay. I used to play with it as a child, during the long silent afternoons when my mother was resting, and only now do I see how badly it was made, for the edge of the border was rough and slightly raised and it should have been as smooth as silk.

When I am in these moods, the best person to be with is Olivia, whose moral strength never falters and in whose company I steady myself, perhaps for the next onslaught, perhaps for the germ of an idea that I can write about when I get home in the evening. She is my only critic. But I think she condemns my hard-won frivolousness.

As I have said, I felt intrigued, excited, by the awesome match between Nick and his wife. They came in carelessly, laughing and absorbed, and at first sight, and indeed on further understanding, they seemed to me to be a single phenomenon. It was only later that I saw Alix as separate, and when I first perceived that she had a personality of her own I also perceived that this personality was not only anterior to her life with Nick but superior to it as well. In our dark and serious room, like a nursery for grown-up children, Olivia and I were drinking coffee out of mugs with suitably juvenile decorations. Women in their places of work frequently give way to these domestic impulses and festoon their offices with pot plants and alternative shoes and the odd cardigan: Miss Morpeth, my predecessor, had her own bone china cup and saucer and a padded velvet coat hanger, and I put these details into my story, which Olivia thought was rather tasteless. Being unmarried and childless, and still living in our parents' houses, Olivia and I don't go so far as to create a home away from home; we limit ourselves to our Mickey Mouse mugs, over the rims of which our eyes scan the Library and each other, meeting in a mutual warning gaze when anything disruptive or subversive seems about to happen. It was in such a gaze that our eyes became locked when we heard that laughter outside our door, presaging our introduction to Alix.

She was not beautiful but she had such an aura of power that she claimed one's entire attention. She was tall and fair, with rough streaky hair and rather small grey eyes which disappeared when her magnificent mouth opened in one of those laughs that I came to know so well. The mouth, and everything about it, was her most important feature: the long thin lips, the flawless teeth, the high carrying voice. We saw and understood Nick's delight when he inspired her to laughter and the head went back and the mouth stretched and the sound, which was in fact rather swallowed and restrained, rewarded him. The brilliance of that laughing face, with the careless hair and the rapacious teeth, was the exact complement to Nick's roving unplatonic gaze, indicating immense reserves of appetite and pleasure. She left one in little doubt that it would be an honour to engage her attention.

They seemed to be in incessant physical union; he held her hand or put an arm round her shoulder or sought her eye, which held his quizzically, the eyebrows raised. There was an unspoken dialogue between them, which they occasionally suspended in order to range round for further topics of interest or amusement. She looked speculatively at Olivia, who blushed, and then at me, and I was heartened, at that early stage in our acquaintance, to note the raised eyebrows and the smile, as I put down my mug and stood up. I stood up instinctively, half wary, half welcoming, entirely deferential.

'We were having an argument,' she said, as if she had known me for years, or as if she thought any formalities a waste of time. 'I think my hair would look better swept up, but Nick is dead against it. What do you think?'

I hardly knew what to say, but there was no need for me to speak because Nick was already protesting.

'Darling,' he said, 'you know I like it the way it is. It was like that when I first met you. You can't want to change it.'

She laughed. 'I'm bored with it. Anyway, you never want anything to change. Just let me show you. No, don't say anything yet.'

And she slipped out of her fur coat, which she threw over the back of a chair, disarranging a pile of photographs, planted her bag on my desk, took out a handful of combs and hairpins, and piled her abundant hair on top of her head. When it was sufficiently anchored, she turned to me for my verdict.

'I think it looks very nice either way,' I said lamely, but that didn't seem to matter either because she had already turned to Nick and posed with one hand on her hip and the other smoothing up the escaping strands at her neck. Mrs Halloran and Dr Simek had suspended their research and were looking on as if some voluptuous cabaret had been devised for their entertainment.

'Darling,' Nick protested again, 'you must do as you like, of course, but you know how I feel about it. Couldn't you just leave it? Just to please me?'

By this time she was gazing into a small hand mirror, turning her head from side to side to gauge the effect. I tried to look as if this were the sort of thing that usually went on in libraries. I could feel Olivia's disapproval and I knew instinctively that I wanted to dissociate myself from it. I was surprised by Nick's pleading tone, but supposed that it was part of some erotic understanding, an idea which intrigued me.

'H'm,' she said, when she had finished her inspection, which took rather a long time. 'Well, I'll work on it. As for you,' she added, turning to Nick, 'you like it your way all the time, don't you? Every time, in fact,' and she laughed at him, poking him with her finger, and saying, 'Yes? Yes?', at which point Dr Simek pursed his lips

48

and returned his eyes to the folder in which he kept his notes. Mrs Halloran continued to stare unabashed. Olivia picked up a photograph and began to trim it carefully with a pair of scissors.

As she snapped her bag shut, Alix turned to me and said, 'Which one are you?'

I said, 'I'm Frances, and this is Olivia', but she took no notice, and it was then that she invited me to taste her famous spaghetti, adding, inevitably, that she had come down in the world. I got out my diary but she waved it aside. 'I never know what day it is,' she said. 'Come tomorrow. Darling, are we doing anything to-morrow?'

Dr Simek looked up, and Nick's face took on an exaggerated look of pain.

'I know, I know,' he said. 'We were going to have that talk, weren't we, Joseph? But it would be better if you read my article first, you know. So what about some time next week?'

'I have . . . ' began Dr Simek.

But he was interrupted by Alix, who had put on her coat and was demanding to know where she had put her gloves. Had she left them in the restaurant? If so, he would have to go back for them.

'Hopeless, my husband,' she confided to Mrs Halloran, who, I was surprised to note, stared back at her unblinkingly, withholding the approval that I was so eager to offer.

'That's that, then,' she said, once the gloves were found. 'We'll see you tomorrow. Nick will tell you the way.' And immediately she switched her attention to Nick, looking into his eyes and dazzling him with the slow dawning of her smile.

There was quite a silence after they left. I had remained standing all this time, and as I slowly sat down again, I could hear them laughing on the other side of the door. I could even hear her say, 'Well, don't tell me I don't do my duty.' Then Nick murmured something, and she replied, her voice unmodulated from its usual carrying resonance, 'Yes, but darling, *what* a crew. The things I do for England. Frances, did you say that girl's name was? I seem to have asked her to dinner. What's the matter with the other one?' And then her voice died away and after a minute or two I heard the front door close behind them. Olivia, who had kept her eyes on her work throughout this episode, said nothing. Her initial blush had faded, leaving a startling whiteness.

'Well, girls,' said Mrs Halloran, after a pause so total that we could even hear traffic noises from the opposite side of the square, 'I hope you were paying attention. That's how to treat a man, if you ever get one, which I doubt, in this place. You won't get *him*, that's for sure. She has him by the balls.'

This brought us back to reality. Olivia, without raising her voice, suggested that Mrs Halloran might be happier working in the Westminster Public Library. Dr Leventhal appeared in his doorway, glasses in hand, and asked if by any chance we were finding ourselves at a loose end. If so, there was some filing to be done in the basement. Dr Simek, who had closed his eyes, during this last pronouncement of Mrs Halloran's, succumbed to what was clearly an expensive temptation, fitted a yellow cigarette into his long old amber holder with the gold ring round it, lit it with an equally ancient lighter, and inhaled deeply. Mrs Halloran, her face mottled and moody, remained staring straight ahead, her onyx rings beating a steady tattoo on the table. 'All right, all right,' she said, as Dr Simek turned to her with his usual courtesy. 'I've got work to do too, you know.'

'I should make a start on it,' observed Olivia pleasantly. 'We've wasted enough time today already.'

And somehow the afternoon returned to normal and

resumed its unhurried course. The afternoon gradually slipped over the edge that connects it with the daytime and began to offer intimations of the evening to come. I was working on Van Gogh's self-portraits at the time, I remember, trying to disentangle the sequence that he painted when he was either becoming mad or had already gone mad. I was doing this very conscientiously, matching up extracts from the letters and typing them carefully on to slips of paper which I attached to the mounts. I tried to take a detached and efficient interest in what I was doing, but at some point I became aware of the painter's small crafty blue eye staring back at me from its scarlet setting. I felt no sympathy. On the contrary, I felt a spurt of dislike for him, with his workman's clothes and his silly fur hat. My feelings were all for his benighted brother, trying to be a respectable art dealer in Paris and having to cope with this nutter and his demands. I try to raise a small cheer for sanity, from time to time. We rationalists must fly the flag, you know.

I distributed tea all round, that day, for we were all a little unsettled. But if the others were, for their various reasons, anxious to rid themselves of the impression that the Frasers had made, I was not. I went over it again and again in my mind. And when I walked Olivia to her car that evening, I did not linger. I did not stop for coffee, as I usually did, but sped home with great strides of excitement. When Nancy had locked the door behind me, as she always did unless I told her that I was going to be out, I sniffed the dull muffled air of the flat, I prepared to face the ritual tray of ritual food, I knew that all this was intolerable, and I tolerated it because I had been offered a glimpse of the world outside. I would see how the others, the free ones, conducted their lives, and then I could begin my own.

F O U R

I slipped into the routine of dining with the Frasers, scarcely believing my good fortune. I registered with amazement the fact that Alix seemed to have taken to me, and that Nick accepted my presence in their flat without comment. In fact his face would appear round the door of the Library at about six o'clock in the evening and he would nod and I would pick up my bag and follow him out, aware of Mrs Halloran's speculative eye on my back. I don't think I was forcing my company on them, although I was avid for theirs. In those early days I never telephoned, except to say thank you, and these conversations would lead to another invitation, or rather to an assumption that I had nothing else to do. I was a little shy of confessing my unfilled evenings and always said that I was going to write, to which Alix always replied, 'Oh, well, if that's all, you might as well come round here.' And of course I would always go. I salved my conscience by doing bits of shopping for her, and of course I insisted on paying when we went to the restaurant.

I think they were both glad that I took such an interest in Nick's work, Nick for obvious reasons, and Alix because she got fed up with it, regarded it with pride but also with some resentment, and occasionally behaved as if he were being unfaithful to her when he was actually engaged on it. She had the same attitude to my writing, I soon discovered, although I could not see how this constituted a menace to her peace of mind, and anyway I was only too glad to be relieved of the burden of my solitude – which was what my writing represented – to persevere with it. And yet it was an old habit, to which I returned when solitude reclaimed me, usually late at night, when I was sleepless, and when I wrote my diary these days I had so much more to record, always with a view to my nebulous novel. But I found that this novel, which was supposed to be about the Library and the characters who used it, the odd people whom I used to describe so amusingly to my mother, had been elbowed out of the way by the extraordinary quantity of new information I seemed to be acquiring. I wrote it all down, but I could not see how to use it, for it all seemed to have to do with the Frasers, and how could I possibly use that? Yet around those silent midnights, when the flat in Maida Vale had long been put to sleep, my pen raced over the pages, gaining speed and point from the increased urgency of my absorption in their lives.

As I said, Alix did not like my writing. She regarded it as a secret which I was keeping from her. 'But what do you write about?' she would demand. I could never tell her, not because I was embarrassed about it but because it had as yet no definite shape. I felt that it had to be kept under lock and key until it had resolved itself, which it would do, sooner or later; I was superstitious about letting anything escape. I tried to explain this, but quite clearly I failed to convince her, and she regarded it as a sort of disloyalty. 'Darling,' she would call out to Nick, 'Little Orphan Fanny's holding out on me.' 'Oh, poor baby,' a muffled voice would reply, usually from inside the clean shirt into which Nick was changing, before we all went down to the restaurant. 'Come and make her tell me,' Alix would call out, and she was almost serious. He would come into the sitting room, his sleeves inside his shirt but his chest bare, and I would watch as he went over to her and nuzzled his face in her hair. 'She who must be obeyed,' he would say, and, to me, 'Force yourself. She always gets her own way in the end.' So I would force myself, and with the slightest feeling of betrayal (but this was somehow better than my earlier solitude) I would tell her about the characters – and in the telling they became 'characters' – whom I had intended to put into my novel. I found that when I exaggerated the grotesque nature of their behaviour I could raise a momentary laugh but most of what I told her left her impassive. 'H'm,' she would say. 'Sounds very odd to me. I can't see anybody wanting to read about such a lot of deadbeats.' She read little herself, although their flat was always cluttered with expensive magazines. I can still see Alix flicking disdainfully through the pages, as if unwilling to believe any woman better dressed or more alluring than herself, holding such women at arm's length, and finally flinging them aside in order to renew her nail varnish or to try, once again, to perfect her new hairstyle. This always required Nick's attention, or his final verdict, and as the three of us gathered around her dressing table, making suggestions, persuading or dissuading, the question of what I was writing faded quite naturally into the background. And after a while, when I telephoned, I ceased to use the excuse that I was writing and instead asked her if I could get her anything in town.

She once said, 'If you must write, find something that interests other people. You can't expect them to be interested in a lot of nuts.' I at once became anxious to dissociate myself from these people, although their ghosts lingered distressfully in my mind. 'I'm the one who should be writing a novel,' she continued. 'If you only knew what my life was like before I came down in the world.' And she would tell me about her schooldays in Switzerland, and the years she spent in Paris when she first came into her money, and the beautiful estate in Jamaica to which she returned each winter, to her adoring and handsome father whom she accompanied on his travels and who was so pleased to have such a colourful daughter on his arm. 'People took us for lovers,' she used to say, and she never really got over his death and the news about his impending bankruptcy. 'Poor Daddy,' she said. 'He died just in time.' But she could hardly bear to think of the days when the estate had had to be put up for auction, and although she had managed to salvage some of the furniture and bring it to England, she hated seeing it in its present setting.

I examined this furniture with some respect. I don't know exactly what I expected to see, but it was certainly not these handsome and hefty Edwardian pieces, walnut tallboys and tables, olive green button-backed armchairs and sofas, all crammed into the mournfully regular little rooms of their Chelsea flat. Although I could not admire Alix's furniture, I registered the fact that it had a more distinguished lineage than my own, and I could see why the zig-zag rugs and the wrought-iron lampstandards of Maida Vale had inspired her to mirth. The difference between us was that she clung to her memories and allowed them to overshadow the present, whereas I tried hard to disown mine and looked forward to a time when they would not trouble me. Then I would shed my surroundings, like a butterfly sheds a chrysalis, and I would fly towards a future which was not lumbered with other people's relics. But Alix strove to preserve a past which was not only past but also out of date, since she now had her life with Nick. Sometimes I could feel her weighing them both in the balance, as if ... as if they had let her down. It was difficult for me to understand this, although I could only admire her exigence. Her eyes would narrow when she saw Nick's books on the desk which had once belonged to her father, and she always kept the curtains half drawn because she could not stand the metal window frames, or the view of the houses across the street. Her sitting room was always half in darkness, which seemed appropriate to her tigerish nature. All this I wrote down in my diary.

And the little details too. How her black maid, Melanie, used to wash and iron her nightgown every morning. How the houseboys always poured hot water into the fragile teacups and emptied them and dried them carefully before serving the tea. The beautiful tropical fruits they had for breakfast, on the veranda. 'You can get mangoes in Harrods,' I offered, trying to be consolatory, but she merely tossed her head. And I could imagine her hatred of the cold grey streets and her contempt for Nick's depressed patients, and the impatience of the wealthy sugar planter's daughter as the boring colourless days succeeded each other, with only colourless people like myself to visit her. She seemed to be disappointed in her friends as well, in some indefinable way. And I, who was merely a latter-day recruit, felt permanently on probation.

Yet I was in my way necessary. I was an audience and an admirer; I relieved some of her frustration; I shared her esteem for her own superiority; and I was loyal and well-behaved and totally uncritical. Yet she found me dull, intrinsically dull, simply because I was loyal and well-behaved and uncritical. And I knew that she would always prefer people like her friend Maria, whom she could insult and scandalize, whom she would defame and snub, only to have it all done back to her by Maria. This provided her with a sort of excitement which I found rather tedious. Nick and I would be greeted with a furious account of what Maria had said about her to a mutual friend, one of those friends whom she telephoned every day. 'I'll never go near that bitch again,' she would pronounce, usually on the evenings when I had arranged to take them to the restaurant. Then Nick would ring up Maria, and plead with her, and the telephone would be handed to Alix, who would shout, 'You cow!', and after a lengthy and accusatory riposte from Maria she would shut her eyes and dissolve into her secret and hedonistic internal laughter, and we would go down to the restaurant after all, about an hour and a half later than usual, and I would have my way over the bill.

What interested me far more, although I also found it repellent, was their intimacy as a married couple. I sensed that it was in this respect that they found my company necessary: they exhibited their marriage to me, while sharing it only with each other. I soon learned to keep a pleasant noncommittal smile on my face when they looked into each other's eyes, or even caressed each other; I felt lonely and excited. I was there because some element in that perfect marriage was deficient, because ritual demonstrations were needed to maintain a level of arousal which they were too complacent, perhaps too spoilt, even too lazy, to supply for themselves, out of their own imagination. I was the beggar at their feast, reassuring them by my very presence that they were richer than I was. Or indeed could ever hope to be.

Alix would break from Nick's embrace, laughing, leaving him flushed, and turn to me, and remark, 'She's blushing! We've shocked her!' And I would smile pleasantly and noncommittally, and she would throw herself into a chair and light a cigarette and say to Nick, 'We must do something about her. Darling, you must know some men. Find her a man, or something. Can't you find someone for Fanny? She'll grow cobwebs just sitting here with us. She'll get bored.' And Nick would say, 'I know, I know', with his comic guilty look, the one he used when Dr Simek waylaid him, and I would smile at them, hoping, in spite of my resistance to this display, that they sincerely wanted me to share as they shared and be happy, and that somehow they would make our party of three into a party of four, that they would cause there to be two couples, and we would be equals at last. I discounted their cruelty as a by-product of their excitement. I know that euphoria, that mania, that love and carelessness breed. And because I longed to experience it again on my own account, and not just to watch it, I had to trust them.

'But first of all we must do something about your appearance,' Alix would say, and this meant sitting me down at her dressing table and dabbing at me with blushers and eye shadows and then turning me round and showing me to Nick. He would reward me with his hard, speculative gaze, which brought more colour to my cheeks, although when I was turned round again to inspect myself in the mirror I would be horrified to see my clean brown face so smudged, and as I watched my new slightly crooked dark red lips utter some words I was quite surprised that my new enlarged eyes could register such pain. I became quite firm on the matter of my appearance, and wiped and scrubbed all the colour off, raising my dripping face in their bathroom to find Nick leaning curiously against the door jamb. I would brush past him and go back into the bedroom to do my hair, only to find Alix at her dressing table, turning her head from side to side to study the back of her neck, anchoring her chignon with pins and combs, settling her pearl studs in her ears, and stubbing out her cigarette. Myself quite forgotten.

They were essentially amorous, teasing, arousing, withdrawing. It had become second nature to them, as had their satisfactions and their occasional boredom. Since I had long ago cast myself in the role of an observer, always with my writing in mind, I observed, but always with little shocks of either pleasure or disappointment. I observed their areas of tolerance and intolerance, their favours offered and just as abruptly withdrawn. I found myself striving to capture their attention, their good will. I knew that I could lose all this quite easily, simply because I was so predictable, so consistent. So bourgeois, as Alix would say, not troubling to hide from me the fact that this was the supreme condemnation. I see no harm in the bourgeois way of life, myself. I like regularity of behaviour and courtesy of manner and due attention paid to the existence of other people. I like an ordered life and discretion and reliability. And honesty. And a sense of honour. But I am aware that all these things have little currency where matters of love and friendship are concerned, and that an attractive shamelessness is a good passport to social success. Much better value, as Alix agreed, when I once said some of this to her.

And yet they had a sort of regard for me, or perhaps it was a tolerance, an acquired taste, a novelty. They cast me in the role of their apprentice, and as such they looked after me. They would never, for example, allow me to take a taxi, when we left the restaurant; they always insisted on driving me home. Alix would question me persistently about my love affairs, my income, my desires, and I would answer her in all simplicity. And yet I would see her turn with evident relief to the roaring ritual insults she exchanged with Maria. Maria, in her way, was a critic. Maria sharpened her up. And when Alix had a fight on her hands, an intrigue, a speculation, she was released from the cold grey boredom, in which ambiance I so clearly belonged.

They soon became an addiction, to which I gave myself, aware that it was precarious but also aware that it was more fruitful than my regular orderly life, with its bourgeois preoccupations, that it yielded more company, more excitement, than I could hope to find on my own. Sometimes it left me a little sad, and the images would resurface, and the images would be of a resignation and of a patience with which I had always been impatient. I would exchange the burden of my memories and of Nancy and Dr Constantine and Dr Simek and all the other doctors that I looked at every day (Goya's Dr Arrieta would come into my mind) for the haphazard and impromptu and exciting company of the Frasers, for their restlessness and their cruelty and their kindness. I took, as they say, the rough with the smooth. I could no longer think of life without them.

As for Maria, I found her oddly restful. She was pleasant to me in an offhand but perfectly polite manner and accepted me, always with a formal handshake, before turning her attention to Nick and Alix, with whom she shared the same callous and unselfconscious jokes. I regarded her as an adjunct to their life which I did not resent, and which did not even interest me very profoundly. I got on with my dinner, handing them over to her in my mind; their quarrels and teasing raged over my head while I gathered strength for further study. And of course I wrote it all down.

The restaurant was always crowded, always full of noise and smoke. Voices rose, jokes were shared between tables, new arrivals greeted with mockery or acclaim. Everybody knew each other or about each other. An indecent sort of honesty prevailed and I soon knew the secrets of every couple or threesome; I discounted these as irrelevant to my enquiry and let the provocative comments go past me. I was a little surprised at their lack of reserve, and at Alix's persistent questioning. But they seemed to find it normal, and perhaps it was. Certainly

60

they seemed to enjoy it. It had the liberating and unsettling effect of one of those encounter groups, in which people are encouraged to criticize each other, or confess, and from which they are supposed to gain a strength to live more realistically. Certainly there was an undercurrent of brutality there, but not, oddly enough, of hostility. People were accepted, sins or crimes forgiven or indulged, disloyalties understood. Occasionally there would be a quiet night, when nobody much turned up, and I was surprised to note how the conversation languished. Maria would sit at our table, and she and Alix would exchange only desultory remarks, yawning from time to time. Nick never said much, after his initial greeting of Maria. She, in turn, treated him with enormous respect, as indeed everyone else did, and spoke reverently about his work. But those quiet nights were quite outdistanced by the noisy ones, when the laughter rose and the faces became flushed and there was a marvellous feeling of masks being cast aside and politeness abandoned. Collusion, complicity, the honour that is said to obtain among thieves: these were what delivered me from my rigidity and my fearfulness, for I hoped to become like one of those friends, my new models.

And those nights delivered me from the ones I used to spend, with Nancy's silent offering on a tray, sometimes watching television with her in the kitchen. Those early, lonely nights, when I habitually went to bed too soon and got far more sleep than I needed. And when the only noise was the sound, far below, of the lift gates clashing, but no step along the corridor, no one coming to our door. We had no visitors, for the old order was maintained. And it was the old order from which I had been delivered, and I sat thankfully in the smoky noisy restaurant and I got far less sleep than I needed, and all this I owed to Nick and Alix.

Who also, when they wished, delivered me from Sundays. Sunday was a day I had dreaded for as long as I can remember, a day given over to silence, and to 'resting', to long walks, and visits to the National Gallery. When my mother was alive, the day had had a certain sweetness. Nancy would change into her dark blue dress, and the three of us would eat lunch together in the dining room, at that baronial table. The two women would retire, after this lunch, and the silence would become even denser, as if all the clocks had stopped. I would walk for two or three hours, until it was time for tea, which Nancy would bring in on one of her trays; my mother would be a little restored after her rest, and that is when I would read to her what I had been working on.

But recently Sundays have been a burden. I could hardly ask Nancy to sit with me at that table; she would think it improper for me to take over my mother's functions, for she still regards me as a child. So I usually go out. Nancy never goes out unless she has to, and I feel that on Sundays she should have the flat to herself. Sometimes I go to my Aunt Julia, my father's sister, but I don't care to do this too often because she always wants to discuss stocks and shares and I really can't get interested in money to the extent of moving it around, as Julia does. Sometimes I go to friends of mine in the country, very old friends, a married couple whom I am beginning to find rather dull. I suspect that they feel the same about me. Usually I go round to the Benedicts, Olivia's parents. They have always been immensely kind and I suppose that I feel at home there, although their home is very different from my own. Olivia's mother was made a Life Peer by Harold Wilson and talks about nothing but the Labour Party. Olivia's father is a comfortable but retiring sort of man, a company lawyer by profession. Olivia's brother David is a doctor and he got us our jobs at the Library; it has always been assumed (and indeed greatly hoped by my mother) that David and I will marry. Lunch at the Benedicts' is a brisk and chatty affair which always ends in a furious cracking of brazil nuts; the food is indifferent, which surprises me in a Jewish family. But I like being there and I am very fond of them all; it is just that I know I have to leave them to an afternoon together, for they are very devoted and hardly see each other during the week, and that is when I go to the National Gallery or the British Museum or the Tate. When I walk home, it seems to me that the hour between five and six is the saddest hour of the week.

So that to be rushed up the motorway in Nick's car, with Alix singing rude songs in the back, is a distinct improvement. The intention is always to take a healthy walk, or to visit a friend, or to find a place for tea, but we never seem to get out of the car, or when we do Alix finds it too cold, so the walk never materializes. But the tea safari has become very amusing. We pretend to be inspectors from some food or hotel guide, and when we have eaten, Alix insists on interviewing the manager or the manageress. She has this gift of bringing people out, and going home in the car she mulls over the information and makes us laugh with her comments. But sometimes she gets one of her sudden moods of boredom and falls silent, thinking, no doubt, of Sundays in Jamaica as the grey unspectacular suburbs unfold and we come back to London. I sense then that they want to be together, and I leave them. Nobody goes to the restaurant on Sundays, so I spend the evening alone. But by this time I have more to write about, so it doesn't really count.

One dread Sunday every month I visit Miss Morpeth, my predecessor at the Library, now retired and living in a very warm flat in Kensington. It has fallen to my lot to visit her once a month, to see how she is getting on; I have somehow been voted into this activity by the staff at the Institute, who seem to think that I am good with old people. The matter was mysteriously decided one afternoon during my absence at the dentist's, and when Dr Leventhal put it to me, I was so relieved to be back at my desk that I agreed. The sad thing is that these visits give no pleasure either to myself or to Miss Morpeth, who would be more gratified by a visit from Dr Leventhal, or, best of all, from Nick, on whom she dotes.

Miss Morpeth has all the unseemliness of a plain elderly woman in not very good health. I hear her limping to the door and unfastening all the locks and bolts which she deems essential for her protection. I follow her down the corridor, noting her elastic stocking, her thinning hair, her yellow neck. She wears sad green skirts with matching cardigans, amber beads. On her right hand, her mother's wedding ring. She seems sealed off from the vital interests of the living world, and I think she dislikes me, not only because I have succeeded her, but because I am young, because I can walk without pain, because I am not humiliated by my body. Miss Morpeth is a conscientious woman and she tries to overcome this hostility, which shames her. Every time I come she prepares a nursery tea of bread and butter, cut very thin, and jam, followed by Battenberg cake. This is ready on a trolley in the kitchen and all I have to do is wheel it into the sitting room, while Miss Morpeth raises the kettle in one careful hand – a red hand, with almost anatomically blue veins – and pours water which has boiled once or twice, so great is her anxiety for me to have come and gone, into her mother's china teapot.

When she is settled in her chair, and she has asked me her ritual question – 'Would you like your cake first or your bread and butter?' – and the business of teacups and plates is settled, and later, when she has lit up her cigarette with the gold lighter we all gave her when she left, we turn to the matters of the day. There is a ritual to be observed here too. She asks about attendance figures in the Library, about the intake of new material in the various categories, about Dr Leventhal, questioning me closely on his ability, for he was not a favourite of hers, and finally on the subject closest to her heart: Nick's career. She is passionately interested in this, and his visits to the Library were the highlight of her day: she would abandon everything to help him, struggling with folders of photographs until he would take her quite firmly by the shoulders, turn her round, and march her back to her desk. He was very sweet to her, and he brought Alix to the little party we gave her when she retired. I vaguely remember him introducing them to each other, although that was before I really knew her. I remember Nick saying, 'Now you can do whatever you want', and then turning away to get Alix a glass of sherry. They promised to visit her, and said they hoped to see her as often as she could put up with them, but I don't think they ever have. And frankly, as I sit in her stuffy room, eating the bread of affliction, bread that we do not really want to share with each other, I sense their reluctance to enter this other kingdom of the shades, and I condone it.

The ritual is pursued in its accustomed fashion. After I have told her that Nick and Alix are well (and felt uncomfortable in doing so, for though my interest in them is justified, I do not care to think of hers) I ask her about her forthcoming visit to Australia. Miss Morpeth made sensible plans for her retirement by announcing her decision to take a long trip to visit her niece in Melbourne. We all agreed that this was the best thing for her, since she had been finding the winters increasingly taxing and sometimes had difficulty in walking without a stick. After some delay the project has ripened to the point of no return, and I discuss with Miss Morpeth the best place to buy lightweight luggage, although how she is to carry anything at all I do not know. 'I intend', says Miss Morpeth, with the air of one yielding

65

to a dangerous impulse, 'to take Nick up on his kind offer to drive me to the airport.' 'Of course,' I agree. 'He will be only too delighted.'

After this exchange, the visit is to all intents and purposes over. I wheel the trolley back into the kitchen and insist on doing the washing up. This takes much less time to do than it takes Miss Morpeth to dry the fussy cups and arrange them on hooks in the kitchen cupboard. She never asks me how I am. She was quite kind when my mother was ill, but maybe she feels I no longer need kindness. Maybe she resents me even more profoundly than I know. I always forget that she hates being kissed goodbye until it is too late and she has drawn back in affront. I always, like a child, kiss everybody, or offer my face to be kissed, and it gives me a tiny shock when faces are turned away from me. Then I leave. Something makes me wait outside the door while the chains and locks are activated for the evening, and then I bound down the stairs with an energy made more frantic by the thought of Miss Morpeth sitting down to her usual Sunday task of writing to her niece. By the time I reckon she has placed the comma after 'My dear Angela', I am down four flights of stairs and halfway to the bus stop.

For by this time I am tired of being serviceable and being sensible and I begin to resent this call on my time. I am anxious to leave Miss Morpeth, even anxious to get home. This time of the year, when the leaves drift silently down, and the nights draw in, always makes me melancholy. I think with longing of the Frasers, but I know that this is the time they like to spend together, and so I never telephone. The evening passes somehow; I watch television with Nancy, or I write. It is difficult, not having a family, and it is also difficult to explain. I always go to bed early. And I am always ready for Monday morning, that time that other people dread.

66

F I V E

That was how my new life started, and I was delighted with it. It seemed to me then, and it seems to me now, that the Frasers were introducing me to, and even instigating, a form of further education from which I could not fail to benefit. I became sharper, funnier, more entertaining. I made the Library into a sort of serial story for Alix, for Nick had confided to me, once when we were driving down Sloane Street, that she sometimes got rather depressed and that it was up to us to divert her and to ward off those moods when she remembered Jamaica, and her father, and would sound off about the awful metal windows and the cramped kitchen of the flat off the King's Road. But at the same time it seemed to me that Alix's depression was of a recognizable and tolerable sort, the sort with which Nick, as a doctor who specialized in these things, should surely be able to deal. It was, essentially, a depression that could be cured, a depression that might vanish at the prospect of a new attraction or entertainment, a depression, in short, that I was inclined to reclassify as plain boredom. I knew enough about the work done at the Institute to realize that true depression, the figure of Melancholia with her torn book, is another matter altogether. Really hopeless people do not expect miracles, nor do they manage to summon up the energy to look for them.

In any event I kept this to myself, for I learned very quickly that I must never criticize. For happy and successful people, Nick and Alix were extraordinarily sensitive to criticism, and I learned not to look askance at her when she claimed to have come down in the world or complained of Maria or even of Nick, whose work occupied a good deal of his attention, attention which she thought should have been devoted entirely to herself. I can see now that she was not only restless but even dismayed by the lack of continuous satisfaction which her present life provided. It was for this reason that her attention seized on gossip, on intrigue, and, if none were to hand, usually through the agency of Maria, she would interrogate strangers, whom she thought looked interesting, and try to find out the central drama of their lives. We had certain discussions about this, for I maintained that dramas in a life took a long time to mature, that every life was of its essence dramatic, but that careful study was needed to perceive such dramas, either in the making or in the sad disappearance. But she insisted that I was wrong; some lives, she said, were more interesting than others, and most could be discounted. What she wanted was a drama that would last until something else claimed her attention, one that would fill an empty afternoon, or a week, or, at the very longest, a month. Her anecdotes were of a violent or sensational character, as if all the mediating information had been removed. 'But he can't just have dropped dead,' I would protest, when she told me about her father, or, 'How do you know she never spoke to him again?' when she offered her account of Maria's divorce. 'Nonsense,' she would say. 'You don't know what you're talking about, Fanny. You just don't know what makes people tick. How could you, working in that place and living in that morgue?' There was no answer to this, and after a time I would cease to contradict her. When she claimed to have talked a woman out of a suicide attempt – a woman she had encountered in the supermarket, in tears – and that this woman, after suitable advice, had gone home in a totally different frame of mind, I said nothing. What could I say? I did not doubt that her assurance and her gusto could have an inspiring effect. And, thinking of Miss Morpeth, I certainly had no victories of my own to place in the balance.

So I learned to divert her, for, during a period when Nick was very busy and inclined to be late home, I took to making my own way over in the evenings, crossing the park in the fine autumn dusk. It was on those evenings, when I would stay with her until Nick came home, that I would tell her about the people in the Library, turning them into characters, making them broader and more extreme than I should have done had I been talking to my mother, or Olivia. As I intended, in my new life, to dispense with shadows, I made them all very clear-cut, and found them much more amusing that way. This served two purposes: it was a rehearsal for the workings of my novel, and it kept Alix from talking about money, which she tended to do when out of spirits, contrasting her past with her present circumstances. Although I could not see that the Frasers had ever lacked for money, although indeed they seemed to spend a great deal, I did see that her anxiety was genuine.

It was at moments like these that she would speak to me of letting the spare room, preferably to myself. The idea was overwhelmingly attractive to me. A move from Maida Vale would be symbolic; it would signify a complete break with the old sad way of life. I could walk out on the zig-zag rugs and the creaking hide chairs and the china and glass birds with as little sense of remorse as if

I had never seen them before; they would be left to the next tenant and in that way I would not feel a pang of sorrow at seeing my parents' flat dismantled. Nancy could be dispatched to her sister in Cork, which would be appropriate, for I must admit that I did not look forward to her inevitable decline. She had been there at the beginning of my life; I did not want to witness the end of hers. I need bring nothing away with me. And there would always be company at the Frasers'. If I moved in with them I would be delivered from the silence of Sundays, and all those terrible public holidays – Christmas, Easter – when I could never, ever, find an adequate means of using up all the available time.

I find, however, that this particular dilemma, which I will call Public Holiday Syndrome and which I would rank next to Two-Star Hotel Bedroom Syndrome as an affliction to which I am particularly prone, is not to be talked about, even as a joke. It is generally felt that complaints about loneliness are unseemly and should be turned over to professional samaritans. My own friendships have always been strong, but they no longer satisfy me. I do not seek out friends so that they will offer consolation: I have a horror of that. I am an extremely good listener, and thus pretty well in demand, although recently I suppose I have been lazy. I have been aware of a boredom, a restlessness, that no ordinary friendship can satisfy: only an extraordinary one. I have grown tired of my lot, I suppose, and have wanted strenuously to change it. So I write, and I take a lot of long walks, and I ferment my ideas, and if I am lucky they come out as vivid as I should like real life to be. That may indeed be the purpose of the exercise. It just tends to break down at times like Good Friday or in places like dim foreign hotels. Then, the lure of company, any company, is enormous, and I feel it might be more sensible to prepare myself for contingencies like these by accepting the sort of offer that Alix was now making.

The only thing that made me pause before finally committing myself was the thought of my novel waiting to be written. I knew that I would have to pay for the company of Alix and Nick with the surrender of all my free time; I knew that Alix would look on any withdrawal from their society with suspicion, and that Nick would consider me thoughtless if I left Alix on her own for any evening on which he might be late home. In short, if I were to consider myself a writer, then I was ideally situated in that warm silent flat in Maida Vale, with Nancy in the kitchen. She was not really a burden to me, nor was I a burden to her; we shared the same food, we knew each other's habits and movements, we were allied by the same memories and associations. At Christmas, that time when we were both a little forlorn, I knew she would be desolate if she had to tell Sydney Goldsmith, who always paid a seasonal visit, that she was being moved back to Ireland. The image sprang up in my mind: Sydney proffering his lavish box of chocolates, Nancy in tears, a lace handkerchief of my mother's (for I gave her most of the things) pressed to her mouth. I could not quite dismiss this image, although I had conjured it up. It did not strike me until much later that this scene, which was so vivid to me, had not yet taken place. I saw no significance in the fact that this episode, pieced together from elements observed at disparate moments (the box of chocolates from many previous occasions, the tears from yet another), seemed to be a memory but was in fact a conjuration. The fact that two sets of time had come together in this way I accepted as perfectly normal.

Moreover, I needed my peace and quiet for a little while longer, for I had just finished a short story – a rather amusing one, about Dr Leventhal's disastrous adventures on a Hellenic cruise – and had, on an impulse, sent it off to a prestigious American magazine. I needed to be alone, not only when it came back, as it surely would, but in case, just in case, I should be encouraged to write another. I would have to keep all this to myself, until I could produce the magazine, with my name in it, which was what I dreamed of doing, for with the sanction of public recognition I could gain some allowance of free time in which to write. I knew that it was hopeless to rely on intentions and ambitions. The Frasers could only understand success. Their sympathies were with the successful, not the unsuccessful, with the moneyed rather than with the poor, with the fortunate rather than with the unlucky. And besides, they liked action, speed, gratification, which I could not yet give them. I would have to bide my time.

There seemed to be no urgency. Alix rather liked to discuss the contingency of letting the room, not necessarily to me but to anyone; indeed, it was her favourite form of imaginative exercise. She was extremely good at practical arrangements, and seemed able to dispose of anybody's random or unfinished business, their previous contracts, their future plans, with an efficiency that amounted to *brio*. Any definite decisions were usually obviated by the arrival of Nick and the discussions about where to have dinner, although as we usually went to the same place these discussions were about as academic as the ones about letting the room. But it is sometimes necessary to entertain the fantasies of others, or even to sit still while they entertain their own, so I usually switched off at about this point, making a mental note to myself to switch on again when my co-operation might really be needed.

But one evening, when I arrived in the King's Road after my walk across the park, I found Nick already at home, and with him Dr Anstey, the other brilliant hope,

72

the 'handful' marked out by Mrs Halloran's percipient eye. I remember that it was a Monday and that I had not seen the Frasers since the previous week. I found the three of them in heated conversation, and I was rather surprised and not too pleased to have our original intimacy broken up. I knew Dr Anstey from the Library, but there was little chance to say more than 'Good morning' there, for his visits were as rapid, decisive, and tight-lipped as Nick's were charming and extravagant and discursive. Dr Anstey, who favoured a pharmacological approach to everything, seemed to me to have an abnormally retentive attitude towards his work, and this I compared unfavourably with that of Nick himself, who was full of anecdotes, most of them amusing, although somewhere at the back of my mind I had registered the fact that Dr Anstey was extremely meticulous, and that perhaps if one were ill, perhaps, even, if one were depressed, he would give one his full attention, take one seriously, and not simply see himself as being ... I believe the word is 'supportive'. Not that there is anything wrong with that, of course.

He also struck me as a rather cruel man, although it would have been difficult for me to say why. He was attractive, in a way that did not attract me, and which in any case paled into insignificance beside Nick's smiling charm. He was as fair as Nick himself, but there the resemblance ended, for Dr Anstey's hair, which looked almost gilt against the reddish colour of his face, was worn flat and close to his large elegant skull. I had previously noticed him only in terms of general height and an all-over haughtiness; he had a distinguished air but smiled little and seemed unapproachable. He had a way of looking at one as if demanding a full account of one's progress and credentials; I always found myself working harder when he was around. His general bearing was that of an army officer, just conceivably a leader of men. His features were large but good and so impassive that it was difficult to remember them individually. The eyes were hooded and light blue, and he seemed to look at one from under his eyelids. One's attention was taken by his hands, which were large and angry-looking. In my mind's eye he was always striding about the Library in a long and correctly tailored black overcoat; he always seemed to be there before I arrived, and he never said anything.

I found them looking animated and pleased with each other, and after my surprise I realized that it was only natural that he should be there; he and Nick were, after all, colleagues, even if their approaches were so very different. Without his coat on Dr Anstey was revealed to be wearing an equally correctly tailored grey suit, a white shirt, and a severe blue tie, which threw Nick's pullover and open neck into the pleasantest possible relief. Dr Anstey's face was rather flushed; his voice, which I hardly remembered ever having heard before, sounded deep and rusty, as if he rarely used it.

Alix had obviously found him interesting and with her usual expertise was what my mother would have called 'drawing him out'. I paid particular attention to this because when I try to do it the results are usually disastrous; nobody gives me a straight answer, so I go on and on like some inhumane detective on a murder case. When information breaks down, as it always does, I then turn into a student of form and meaning: I study the sub-text. By this stage, of course, I have all the time in the world to work this out, the subject having flown far, far away ... But Alix was managing brilliantly, her voice light but friendly, her social position legitimating all her questions. She had even got him to tell her about his divorce, although I would have thought that this was the last subject on which he would wish to talk, and this might have accounted for his flushed face, on which embarrassment was mixed with an obvious desire to be agreeable. It struck me that he might have been rather lonely, that his hauteur was a defence, and that he was as delighted to have his privacy violated as I had been. In any event, he was, as the police say, helping them with their enquiries.

Alix waved an arm at me and I slipped out of my coat. I sat down quietly, aware that my function had been altered by this addition to our original group, and feeling my way towards some kind of new status. I knew the moves, you see, the stunning invitations to intimacy, the instant crash of barriers falling. I knew then, and I know now, that this is the only way in which the over-disciplined can be sprung from their trap. I sat back, like the oldest inmate of a prison or a hospital ward, watching the initiation ceremonies being undergone by the latest arrival, eager to congratulate that new recruit on having comported himself correctly, won his spurs, gained his passport to life on the inside. I also observed that for those who undertake the initiation, it is always the first encounter that establishes the transaction, and it is always the barriers that remain – for some barriers always do remain, in spite of the reconditioning – that establish the outcome of the drama, or, to put it another way, the final form of the contract. I thought, with a slight tinge of melancholy, that this drama or contract would be more interesting than the one I had provided, and yet I sensed that Dr Anstey and I had a great deal in common in the way of good behaviour, moral stuffi-ness, and general lack of experience in the wilder and more interesting areas of human conduct.

Alix was laughing gently at his slight unease, and this, of course, made him act rather more boldly than he would normally have done. I could sense him seeking for ways in which to gain her approval. He was not a particularly amusing man, so I did not see how he could

75

entertain her. But he was attractive. Even I could see that. The novelist in me took over for a moment, and I plotted the whole thing out; then I accused myself of the most suspect form of calculation – crude, louche, cynical – and I dismissed the whole fantasy.

Which was just as well because at that point Alix laughed and said, 'But my dear James, you can't live like a monk! This is terrible! You'd better get together with Fanny here.' At which point Nick joined us, and he laughed too, and then I had to, and so did Dr Anstey, and the sight of our determined hilarity sent Alix off into her throaty, strangled giggle that indicated secrecy and pleasure, and Dr Anstey stood up, the smile stiffening on his lips.

'This', said Alix primly, making an effort to control herself, 'is our orphan child. Little Orphan Fanny.'

'Of course, I know Miss Hinton,' said Dr Anstey, and we nodded at each other.

'You may call her Fanny,' Alix went on. 'She is what my nurse would have called a nice sort of girl. And she's got pots of money.'

Nick laughed and groaned. 'Darling,' he protested, 'you're making her blush.' And he put an arm round me and rocked me to and fro. I smiled, although I could feel the blood rising to my cheeks. I should have been used to this, I told myself.

'Now,' said Alix, 'what shall we call you?'

'My name is James,' replied Dr Anstey, who was still standing. I remember noting that he was as tall as Nick, although slightly heavier in build.

'Oh, James is far too stuffy,' said Alix. 'I'll think of something. And you will have dinner with us, won't you? Don't mind my nonsense. I mean well.'

Dr Anstey hesitated only a moment. I could see his mind dwelling on the prospect of midnight oil and then dismissing the thought. 'I'd like that very much,' he said. 'But would you mind if I telephoned my mother?'

They looked at him in astonishment.

'Why on earth do you want to telephone your mother?'

'Well, she was rather expecting me.' They still looked at him uncomprehendingly.

'I live with her, you see. Not far from here, actually. She has a little house in Markham Street.'

By this time Alix had dissolved once again into her laugh, her head thrown back, her eyes closed, her teeth gleaming. The spectacle of Dr Anstey's regular life and habits seemed to have infected her with a joyousness that charged the room with energy, an energy verging on outrage. The writer in me turned over again, scripting that original plot, and then, once again, I shook myself, and, forcing my gaze outwards, perceived the brilliance of the dramatic indigo evening beyond the curtains, the warmth of the fire, the pleasantness of the surroundings, the good humour that was available for anyone who wished to join in. And I did, of course. Wish to join in, I mean. Why pay the price for being outside it all? I was no writer, I decided, dismissing that fictive outcome which was somehow encoded into my imaginings and therefore doubly shameful. I was no writer: I was a criminal masquerading as a librarian.

So I relaxed, and smiled, and, looking at Dr Anstey, saw that he was embarrassed, and determined to help him.

'My name is Frances,' I said. 'But I feel I should call you Dr Anstey.'

Then he smiled too, and said, 'You must call me James, of course. I've often wished you would.'

So we became James and Frances. We all had dinner together that evening. James was introduced to the regulars; he seemed to grasp the rules immediately. He was, after all, a very clever man. I watched him a lot. I saw that he was a little stiff, a little shocked by Maria's exuberance, but that was only to be expected. I saw that he was enthralled by the sheer novelty of the evening, by the possibilities opened up to him by these new friends. I did a lot of watching that evening. I watched the Frasers and their evident amusement at the success of their strategy. I watched their heads come together, their foreheads momentarily touch, the laziness with which they disengaged. I watched, with a touch of sadness, James watching the Frasers. Of course, the spectacle of two people's happiness is always something of a magnet for the unclaimed. When I finally smiled to myself, and looked down, and drank my coffee, and looked up again, I found that James was watching me.

'Where do you live, Frances?' he said. 'Somewhere healthy, obviously.'

'Healthy?' I asked.

'Well, you always look so healthy when you blow into the Library in the morning.'

I laughed. 'That's because I walk to work. I love walking. But it's no great distance. I live in Maida Vale. And I lived with *my* mother, until she died.'

I felt him relax, and my little sadness passed. 'I like walking too,' he said. 'I do quite a bit of it.' At this point we were turned towards each other, and I sensed that Nick and Alix were watching us. 'You've been at the Library some time now, haven't you?' he went on. 'Do you like the work?'

'But you don't know her secret,' Alix broke in. 'She's really a writer. She's writing a novel.'

I protested, but Nick said, 'Don't be an idiot, Fanny. Tell him all about it.'

So I succumbed and said my piece, and made it funny, and he laughed, and Alix called for the bill, and waved me imperiously aside when I insisted that it was my turn, and then James, whom I now thought of as James, with fairly impressive determination, brought out his wallet and put four ten pound notes on the table.

'Well,' said Alix, 'you must be our guest next time.'

'I'd love to,' he agreed. 'This has been so very pleasant. Can I offer you a nightcap somewhere?'

I think perhaps that he had suddenly grown rather impatient with that hothouse atmosphere of intimacy that had so attracted him earlier in the evening. And his legs were so long that he found sitting at a small table rather uncomfortable. And so we found ourselves, somewhat incongruously, in the lounge of a very large hotel in Knightsbridge and sat ourselves round a table surrounded by acres of orange and brown geometrical carpet. There was no one else there but an Italian family chattering in a corner; their small daughter, a beautiful child with big over-tired eyes and tiny earrings, ran round and round, getting more tired, and stopping on her way to gaze at us. Alix offered her an olive from a dish on our table, and she covered her face with her hands and ran back to her mother.

I remember that they were putting up Christmas decorations, two-dimensional gold trees fixed to the fake pilasters.

'Rather early, isn't it?' I remarked to Alix. It was only the third week in October.

'Oh no,' she said. 'They always do it early. Foreign tourists expect it. Anyway, it can't be too early for me. I love Christmas.'

'I don't,' James and I said simultaneously, and looked at each other in surprise.

'I usually spend it with my mother,' he explained. 'We're both divorced and we both dread it.'

'I can't wait for it to be over,' I confessed, not wanting to go into the business of Nancy and our sad little celebration. Public Holiday Syndrome is something you keep to yourself, I thought. I was amazed and enchanted to find a fellow sufferer.

'But you must come with us this year,' cried Alix. 'A whole crowd of us usually gets together. You know practically everyone by now. It's great fun. And it saves cooking.'

'Spaghetti,' murmured Nick, and dodged a glancing blow.

'Boxing Day is even worse,' James continued; he had by now quite lost his original shyness. 'On Boxing Day I am obliged to go for a healthy walk. A very healthy walk.'

Alix groaned. 'On Boxing Day we go to Nick's parents. Don't remind me.'

Nick laughed. 'Darling, they adore you.'

How interesting, I noted. They adore her. If I were in her place, I should adore *them*.

'I usually go to the Benedicts',' I said. 'Olivia, you know. In the Library. Her parents. But it usually ends up in a healthy walk, just the same.'

'Sounds delirious,' Alix broke in. 'What exactly is the matter with that girl?'

I shouldn't have minded the question, although few people ask it. They take Olivia's disability for granted, as she does. She was injured in a car accident when she was about sixteen. She spent a year in hospital, and a further year at home afterwards. She made a good recovery, but she has a certain amount of difficulty walking, although as she is always sitting down this is rarely noticed. What had caught Alix's eye was her neck brace, that cruel pink collar on which her beautiful head so uncomfortably rests. In my mind's eye I remembered her on that day when Nick had brought Alix to the Library and had invited me to dinner. Olivia had blushed at Alix's glance, and then had whitened when forced to witness the performance with the hair. She had picked up a pair of scissors and had begun to trim a photograph; she had had to bring it up rather high into her field of vision and Alix had noted this too.

I also saw Olivia's perfect face, a colourless olive face with eyes so black that the iris and the pupil seemed to be one. I saw the long waving black hair parted in the middle and falling to her shoulders, over the neck brace. It is this face, and her impeccable good sense and balance, that makes me literally forget her movements when she has to get up from her chair. She is so good at her job, such a natural scholar, that it does not matter that she cannot walk round the tables or carry piles of photographs. I do that for her. It works out quite easily, and what I have in physical strength, she has in moral strength. We are dear friends.

I also see her on those Sundays, after lunch and the brazil nuts, when her untidy mother and her silent father, both rather ugly people, seat her in her chair in the drawing room and gaze at her with unsentimental love. They seem more impressed with her beauty than with her disability, and as they have always taken this attitude, which is perfectly genuine, she is singularly uninhibited about her appearance. I don't know what she feels about it, for she never mentions it, and I have long since ceased to notice it. I put down her blush to her love for Nick, rather than to anything Alix had said or done.

'Spinal damage. She manages very well,' said James, for I could not trust myself to answer. Suddenly the surroundings of that hotel, with the geometrical carpet and the gold trees, seemed tawdry, the refuge of people who had no genuine reason to be out. I had already got Olivia's Christmas present, a first edition of *The Ordeal of Richard Feveral*, her favourite novel, and I also saw the smile that would break up her little face when I gave it to her.

81

Alix began to stir, rather restlessly. 'Well, I think we can do better than that,' she said. James and I looked at each other, and after a moment smiled. 'I'll have a word with Maria,' said Alix. 'And let you know. Put yourselves in my hands.' She looked at us speculatively. 'You could do worse,' she added.

It was close to midnight when we got outside. It was a beautiful night, cold and misty, with a yellow moon. I was tired but excited; I had had such an extraordinary evening that I did not want it to end. I wanted, in fact, to walk a little, but discussions were already under way between Alix and Nick about who was to be dropped first. James, obviously. Markham Street was closer than Maida Vale. The car, when Nick opened the door, smelt of cigarettes.

'Oh,' I said impulsively. 'I wish we could walk.'

'We can,' James replied. 'At least, *we* can. I'll walk you home, Frances.'

I turned to Alix and then to Nick, both of whom looked faintly amused.

'I see,' said Alix. 'I see.' She laughed, and we had to join in. And this time I laughed with genuine pleasure and surprise. For the one thing I had not expected was to be written into the plot. I had really not expected that at all.

We parted with promises to ring up the following day, and our voices left an echo in the misty air.

James and I walked in silence until we got to the top of Sloane Street. Everything around us was quiet, but not quiet enough for me. The air was very still, and there was a faint scent of burnt leaves. After a moment I said, 'Do you think we could walk through the park?'

'Of course,' he replied. 'It's what I intended. You're not tired, are you? Could you walk all the way home?'

I think that was the happiest night of my life. We walked in complete silence through the silent park, and it seemed to me that instead of drawing to a close the year was just beginning. Beginnings are so beautiful. Although I am naturally pale, I could feel the blood warm in my cheeks. I drew no conclusion from this, and my instinct was correct. I was not falling in love. Nor was there any likelihood that I might. But I was being protected, and that was something that I had not experienced for as long as I could remember. I was coming first with someone, as I had not done for some sad months past, and in my heart of hearts for longer, much longer.

'They're a remarkable couple, aren't they?' he asked, more to break the silence than anything else.

'Remarkable,' I agreed. 'Wonderful friends.'

So we walked up the Edgware Road, past the nurses' uniforms and the sex shops and the bleary light from the launderette, and after a while he said, 'You're not tired, are you?' and I shook my head, for I could have gone on for ever.

'But how will you get back?' I asked him suddenly, when we were at my door. 'You have no car, and taxis are hopeless around here.'

'I'll walk back,' he replied. 'Goodnight, Frances. I'll see you tomorrow.'

That night I did not bother to write.

S I X

And I did not write for many evenings that followed. In my new security I began to see it all in a different light. I began to hate that inner chemical excitement that made me run the words through in my head while getting ready to set them down on the page; I felt a revulsion against the long isolation that writing imposes, the claustration, the sense of exclusion; I experienced a thrill of distaste for the alternative life that writing is supposed to represent. It was then that I saw the business of writing for what it truly was and is to me. It is your penance for not being lucky. It is an attempt to reach others and to make them love you. It is your instinctive protest, when you find you have no voice at the world's tribunals, and that no one will speak for you. I would give my entire output of words, past, present, and to come, in exchange for easier access to the world, for permission to state 'I hurt' or 'I hate' or 'I want'. Or, indeed, 'Look at me'. And I do not go back on this. For once a thing is known it can never be unknown. It can only be forgotten. And writing is the enemy of forgetfulness, of thoughtlessness. For the writer there is no oblivion. Only endless memory.

So that when I received a congratulatory letter from the prestigious American magazine, and the news that my story about Dr Leventhal's Hellenic adventures would shortly be published, I felt no urge to sit down and write another. Rather the opposite. I looked on my success as the fitting conclusion to a career wrongly chosen, and dangerous in its implications of future effort and loneliness. I could now sign off with a flourish and never write again.

Of course, I was pleased, in a non-essential way. I felt the reward was undeserved because I no longer wanted that sort of reward. But Olivia was pleased, if only because she takes things so much more seriously than I do. And James was delighted. His haughty, horsey face broke into a smile such as I had never seen before when I told him about it. That smile was directed at the magazine, which he held in his hands, and I knew then that I wanted that smile to be directed nowhere but at myself. Look at me, I wanted to say, look at me. That was how and when I found out about writing.

I telephoned Alix, of course, because that is the sort of thing she loves. She gave a shout, and said, 'Hey, hey. We must celebrate.' 'My treat,' I said. 'I should hope so,' was her reply. 'Shall I ask James to join us?' I felt awkward at this point because I had thought of James so much that I could not have enjoyed this little celebration if he had not been there, so I decided to be entirely honest and said to Alix, 'Oh, yes please. Four is a better number than three, don't you think?' Then I wondered if I had offended her because there was a short silence, and she said, 'I think two is the best number of all, myself', and I agreed so fervently that I managed to convince myself that we had been talking about the same thing. Perhaps we had; I shall never know.

Beginnings are so beautiful. I was not in love with James, but now there was something to get up for in the mornings, other than that withering little routine that would eventually transform me into a version of Miss Morpeth, although I had no niece in Australia who might brighten my last years. Nor would I turn into Mrs Halloran, still game, but doomed to hopelessness. No glasses of gin for me, no bottle in the wardrobe of a room in a hotel in South Kensington, no evenings lying on the bed dressed in a housecoat too young and too pink, casting superior horoscopes for those who fear the future. With what thankfulness did I register my deliverance from this dread, which had possessed me for as long as I could remember. I breathed more deeply, slept more soundly, ate more heartily, freed from this weight. Nancy's mumblings and shufflings ceased to bother me, for they no longer represented the shades of the prison house. In fact I began to love her as I had loved her long ago, when, as a child, I ran to her to be kissed, and made up treats for her. I realized that she too must feel isolated, particularly as she was so shy and did not make friends easily. As I swung out of the building one morning, I had a word with the porter, Mr Reardon, and arranged for him to go up to the flat and have tea, when he came off duty. He could sit with Nancy for half an hour, and give her the evening paper, which he always bought at lunchtime, for the racing forecasts. So that Nancy felt a little happier too.

I felt strong, I felt energetic, I felt ... young. I had never felt this before. I had always understood that I would have to assume responsibilities that others found unacceptable. I had been writing the cheques and paying the bills and the tax when I was still in my teens; it was always I who called the doctor. Nancy would ask me to buy her a new dress, a new cardigan. 'Like my blue one, Miss Fan. The one Madam likes.' Every time I looked at her I could see some garment that I had bought either for Nancy, or for my mother, and the sadness of those afternoons, in department stores, all alone, fingering modest nightgowns, opaque stockings, discreet and genteel garments, and taking them home to that claustral quiet, for their inspection. They loved those times. But I hated them. They were a parody of all the shopping I wanted to do. They interfered with my impulse to please myself, so that I might please others.

I had never thought myself interesting to look at, but now I could not help noticing that my eyes were wider, my expression lively with anticipation. I began to study my appearance in the glass. I looked through my clothes and put the dull sensible things on one side. I got rid of the heavy walking shoes, and gave my navy coat to Nancy. I bought a couple of pullovers, and a wool shirt, in light fresh colours, sky blue and white. I resurrected a pale grey dress with a white puritan collar and a black bow at the neck that I had not worn for a couple of years and had folded up and put aside because I thought it looked too elaborate for the sort of life I led. Now, as I examined myself with a franker sort of appreciation, I thought it made me look interesting, almost unusually so. I began to look forward to dressing up for the day that lay before me.

My attitudes in general seemed to have undergone a change for the better, making me less sharp, more receptive. I felt myself sliding deliciously downwards into a miasma of kindliness. I found amusement in my routine at the Library, not the engineered amusement that I had tried to amass for my stories, but genuine human oddness and fascination. I told no one of the change in myself, the sense I had that life was opening up for my inspection, and more than that, for my participation. Mrs Halloran had long since stopped waiting for me to mention Nick's frequent appearances round the door when he collected me in the evenings. I had disappointed her, I know, but I did not wish to share what I had. For it was such a novelty for me to have anything, although from her point of view I was one of the lucky ones, with the flat and my job and my stable income. I could not tell her that I was only just beginning my life, for she would have stared at me, had such a conversation ever taken place, and asked me what had ever stood in my way. I could not tell her that even in defeat, which was how I viewed my life until this moment, there are certain loyalties to be observed. Her lack of sympathy, I felt, would still have been absolute.

Olivia was pleased, although I had said nothing to her. She was pleased for me, because I was happy, although she may have regretted things for herself. She had not only her love for Nick to forget, but also the hope, which our two mothers had silently shared, that I might marry her brother David. I believe my mother said something to Olivia, when she began to get so very ill, although Olivia, being a creature of exquisite delicacy, has never mentioned this to me. But she knows that my mother loved her; she remembers my mother's thin hand caressing her wondrous hair; she feels the loyalty too. Yet she was pleased for me.

I saw James every day. He would linger in the Library until I arrived in the morning, and I would make us both some coffee, which we drank from the Mickey Mouse mugs. And if we were not going to the Frasers, or meeting at the restaurant, he would walk me home in the evenings. I worried that I could not invite him to a meal, explaining that I would have to get Nancy used to the idea, but he said, 'We have plenty of time', and so there was no awkwardness on that score. The days passed swiftly between our early morning meetings and our long walks home. I don't think that anyone noticed anything. James was much more reticent than I was, much more careful. I was cautious because I could not believe my good fortune; when I could believe it, I knew that I should become extravagantly demonstrative. But he had a high level of control, which I suppose went with his professional demeanour; at any rate, it went well with the rusty unused voice and the haughty and impassive face. I found such reticence very exciting. For I knew he cared for me.

We were very shy with each other. I never asked him about his divorce, for I think I sensed that he too wanted to begin again. Because we were so shy – longing for our meetings, but sometimes faltering in conversation – we made sure that we went out with the Frasers a great deal. Those evenings at the restaurant, with James's arm lying across the back of my chair, and Maria sitting down with us – so that we were five – were very precious to me. Alix and Nick made fun of us a little, but we learned to deal with it, as long as we were together. 'Maria,' Alix would say, 'take a look at this. Aren't they sweet?'

'I'm not ...' we would say, simultaneously, but we never pursued it, for James hated these allusions, and I found them tiresome. But evidently we had been brought up by like-minded parents. My mother had always told me to ignore a remark which I found offensive unless someone's honour depended on it. So I always looked at James and laughed at these moments, and, truth to tell, I enjoyed those moments of complicity as much as all the rest.

Secrets, the right to have secrets. We had very few, for although he told me that I knew him better than anyone, I never really felt that I knew him at all. It was our shyness that we had in common, and it was this that Alix mistook for lack of experience. Because of the bond that our shyness created, because it was always re-inforced by those convivial evenings, the walks home from the restaurant seemed to us heightened, more sig-nificant, than an ordinary walk home from work at the end of the day. It was on one of these occasions that I renounced all caution and invited him in, although I knew that Nancy, looking like a mole in the brushed wool dressing gown that I had bought her, would inevitably shuffle in from the kitchen when she heard two sets of footsteps (her hearing is extremely acute) and have to be introduced. But even this passed off well, for she reminded James of his old nanny and he had a very nice talk with her. After that, she took to leaving us little trays, biscuits and coffee in a Thermos flask, as she had for my parents when they were much younger and still went out in the evenings. And it came to be a very sweet routine for me: the long walk home, in the dry cold, the empty streets, the silent entry into the flat, so as not to wake Nancy (for it was sometimes very late), the removal of coats and gloves, the quick embrace. I would slip into the kitchen to collect the tray, and James would go into the drawing room and light lamps and switch on the terrible electric fire with the simulated logs in the fire-place surrounded by pink tiles with blue kingfishers painted on them. We would drag two pale hide foot-stools, with cabriole legs, in front of the warmth and drink our childish drink, and then I would sit on the ground at his feet and he would put his arm round me, and his large authoritative hand would stroke my face and hair. Sometimes we would talk, sometimes just sit together in silence. I think we were so happy that we found this enough.

Even when we were apart I did not feel alone. On Sundays, after lunch with the Benedicts, I would walk through the streets to the National Gallery or the Tate, and I would think of James, who always spent this time with his mother. I would feel no urgency, no longing, simply an unclouded and beneficent energy. I would look in the windows of expensive shops and wonder if the many exotic things that I saw would be suitable for my adornment. This was pure fantasy for I had no intention of buying them. But it was a significant exercise, for it meant that I considered myself worthy, as I had never done before. The change in my consciousness was so bewildering that I looked back on my previous life with a sort of amazed pity. That narrowness, those scruples, that prolonged childhood ... I even, and this is a great test, began to consider journeys I might make, for my own pleasure, without him. I had never been to Greece, and I thought I might now go, some time soon. And I knew that if I went I should enjoy it, as I had never enjoyed a journey before. Because I should have James to come back to. By the very fact of his existence, he had given validity to my entire future.

He had told me, and these facts I lovingly rehearsed as I walked along the Mall, now grey, the gutters filled with dried and scudding leaves, that he had been born in India. His father had been a diplomat and the family had lived abroad, in different postings, for some years. He had grown up in Brazil, in Egypt, before being sent home to school. This excited me and made me want to enlarge my own horizons. I wanted to emulate his familiarity with different continents, with exotic places. It conferred on him a worldliness, to which I deferred. Sometimes I thought that he must find me dull, and once I confessed as much to him. But he laughed and said, 'Dearest Frances. You couldn't be dull if you tried', and kissed me. Yet I felt in him a superiority, a masculine experience, all the more powerful because he did nothing to exploit it. And at the same time, with so much to turn over in my mind, I did not feel too dull myself.

I began to see him as one of those persons whose destiny I had always desired to follow. To be in his company, to hold his hand, to feel his large fingers tighten round my own, made me feel very humble, very fortunate, very chosen. At such times I would steal a glance at his fair, punishingly flattened, hair, at his hawk-like nose, and wonder what he could see in me. I felt that there must be a world of women, beautiful women, waiting for him. When I thought of this my heart would beat a little unsteadily, and my earlier euphoria change into a wonder that had something anxious about it. I felt there was a danger to me in his very excellence. And yet he seemed perfectly contented. I think in all conscience that he was happy too.

Alix, of course, who was immensely interested in the whole procedure, could not believe that this was all there was to it. I could hardly believe it myself. It was not like anything I had ever known before. But I seemed to be unable to explain this to her. Or rather she seemed unable to accept it. Perhaps I was simply at a loss, for suddenly all the available words, scenarios, plots, exaggerations, seemed to have failed me. That was the most extraordinary thing; I was wordless. Yet Alix could not see that this *was* the most extraordinary thing. I could, but she couldn't. She assumed that I was being furtive. 'Darling,' she would call out to Nick, 'she's holding out on me again.' I would laugh, as I always did, although I was making such rapid strides in self-confidence that I thought it time she took James and myself for granted. But as she had introduced us, she felt she had a proprietorial right in the matter, and she would often exercise this. There was, I perceived, a certain feudalism in her attitude; she not only exacted a sort of emotional *droit de seigneur*; she extended this into perpetual suzerainty. Part of me observed this, but there was nothing I could do about it. I had lost the words with which I might once have investigated the matter.

Instead I turned away from her, aware of some area of unfinished business that threatened our friendship, yet unwilling to waste time on this. I had more important things to do. I had James, my life's work, to study. I had to find out what pleased him, what made him laugh, what he liked to eat. And I had to take my time over this. It all needed the most enormous amount of thinking over. In the first place I had to cancel out all the old information, forget I ever knew ... all those sad spoiled things. Caution was needed. I saw that. I had visions of myself at my old merciless interrogations, and shuddered. This time I was going to be innocent, even if it killed me. And I would not take notes. Well, not many. As few as possible.

So I made no demands, brought about no changes. I was uninformative but I was agreeable. I tried to keep the friendship in order. We continued to eat together, at the usual place, because Alix knew and liked it, and, perhaps because of the increasing cold, Alix was becoming distant and a little fretful. One evening, I remember, she took me into the bedroom and said, quite seriously, 'You're holding out on me, aren't you?' And I said, just as seriously, 'No, Alix, I'm not.' 'Do you honestly mean to tell me', she went on, turning her head from side to side and watching her reflection in the mirror of her dressing table, settling the pearl studs in her ears, and smoothing her hair at the back of her neck, 'that you and James aren't having a roaring affair? You must think I was born yesterday.' I said, although it displeased me to do so, that I was not keeping anything from her. 'H'm,' she snorted, by which time Nick had appeared in the doorway, wondering why we were taking so long. His expression was mischievous, but also pleading, and his glance strayed to Alix, who was by now carefully making up her mouth. She who must be obeyed. Then we went back into the sitting room, where the sight of James, in his long, severe overcoat, thrilled me with delight and I forgot the whole incident.

Nothing could spoil my pleasure. Even when I saw

the magazine with my short story in it, folded back to the title page – 'Professor Rosenbaum and the Delphic Oracle' – and on that same page, clearly unread, a round brown ring, as if a mug of coffee had been rested there, I only said, laughing, 'You haven't read my story.' Alix turned her head, her grey eyes vague and distant. 'Oh. Oh, that. No, I haven't', and then, her eyes still vague, 'Are you very cross?' And I laughed again, and said that I wasn't, but that she had better read this one because I wasn't going to write any more. 'In that case,' she said, 'I don't see why you shouldn't take the spare room.'

There was a certain awkwardness about this. Alix held on to the fact that I had said that I could not move in with them because I needed the flat for my writing. Now that I had announced that I was not going to write any more, she refused to see why I could not take the room. But my flat had become very dear to me, and our late silent evenings, sanctioned by Nancy with her buns and coffee, had become very dear to me too. And I knew they meant quite a lot to Nancy, for she had quite ceased to worry about locking the front door, and so, in some symbolic way, the flat had changed, had become my home, as it had never been before. She was acknowledging me as the mistress of the house, and this was another innocent pleasure, for I had never thought of myself in this light. In fact, as we had so much room, and as James was so fed up with living in Markham Street with his mother, who was not half so accommodating about his late returns, I wondered at which point I should suggest ... But I put this idea behind me, for I knew that he might consider this precipitate. Dear James. I found him so ludicrously well brought up, so full of honour, and I treasured these qualities, for after my long claustration I needed something reliable in my life. Otherwise, the change would have been too dramatic. I needed, I suppose, a continuation of respectability, of

94

quietness. I needed to see Nancy's smile, which I had not seen for a very long time, and which now greeted me in the mornings, when our paths crossed. I needed to enjoy her little indulgences, the fresh rolls she brought me back on Sundays, after she had been to Mass, or the nursery puddings that she started to make again. I needed to deserve these things. And I wanted to be spoilt, at the same time, in the way, I suppose, that fortunate young women are spoiled. Or lucky ones. I wanted to be treated like . . . Like a bride, of course.

And yet I did not love James, in the fatal sense. I did more than that. I enjoyed him. I knew about love and its traps. How it starts well, how mistakes are made, how, in moments of confidence or unbearable pain, things are said which can never be unsaid. How caution intervenes, and you behave like a polite friend, aching with the need to renounce that caution, if only to say intolerable things again. How those intolerable things seem to contain the essence of your knowledge of each other, of intimacy. How cruelty comes into it. And terror. Suspicion. How you are bound by those rules of politeness, self-imposed, once again, never to seek out the vital information. How not knowing becomes worse than knowing. How your life becomes devoted to finding out. And how you find out. I knew all that. I never speak of it.

But James was my friend, and I held his hand as confidently as a child holds the hand of its parent. I told him everything, for he loved to hear me, and being so reticent himself, it was an amusement and a diversion for him to hear me rattle on. And I came to know how to make him laugh, and all the funny things that I had been saving up for my diary and my stories I lavished on him, and they became warmer, kinder in the telling. And he knew things too. He seemed to think as much of Olivia as I did, which made me very happy. He told me

95

that Dr Simek had been a very eminent specialist in Prague, and a professor at the University, that his daughter was an actress but that she had joined the Party, and that now she no longer wrote to him. That, more than his exile, was Dr Simek's great grief. He told me that Mrs Halloran had also been on the stage, although in a much rowdier capacity (I suppose I might have guessed that, and I felt a momentary pang of annoyance because I hadn't), that Dr Leventhal was the sole support of his widowed sister, with whom he lived. I asked him about Nick's research, but he did not want to talk shop, and I never asked him about his. I thought, and I was right, I know, that we dealt with each other as each other would have wished. He pleased me all the time.

For I always knew when I would see him. He did not keep me waiting. He did not make me wonder or speculate. This was so unlike the last time, the time of which I never speak. I can only say that everything that had happened then was miraculously reversed, and I embarked on this venture with full confidence. The worst thing that a man can do to a woman is to make her feel unimportant. James never did that. That whole late autumn, which was exceptionally cold and exceptionally dry, favouring our walks, was for me a time of assurance and comfort and anticipation. There were no images in my head. I did not write. I was happy.

Oddly, or perhaps not oddly, when you come to think of it, I wanted nothing more. I had no thought of going on to the next stage, because I was enjoying this one so much. I knew that it would take me a long time to unlearn my lessons, to let down my defences, to find out how to be carefree and trusting. I still kept to my old habits, still lunched with Julia or the Benedicts on Sundays, made an expedition to Harrods to buy a blouse that Nancy had seen advertised in my Sunday paper and wanted to send to her sister in Cork, because I could not easily renounce a way of life that I had known for so many years. I knew that when the time came some sort of transition would be effected, but that even this transition must be carefully lived through. I did not want to hurt anyone – that old reflex. No one must be disinherited. If I did this carefully, I thought, then I would deserve all my happiness. As to that happiness, so nebulous, and yet so focused, I would let James organize that.

Suddenly it became much colder, and a recognition of the season impinged upon me. The Frasers began to talk again of Christmas. I paid less attention to their plans for us all to get together – I did not entirely want to think of this, for it meant that Nancy would be alone – and concentrated on finding wonderful presents for them all. I went shopping, in those same department stores, but this time looking at incredibly expensive and extravagant things: French soaps, jars of Stilton, cashmere pullovers, Carlsbad plums. I did not buy them for I wanted to extend my pleasure. Every lunchtime I would desert Olivia and go window shopping. From being very frugal I now became anxious to spend as much money as possible. I was in a state of euphoria which cancelled every prudent thought I had ever had.

The cold made our walks exhilarating. We huddled together in the starry silence, my hand in James's hand, in his pocket. We strode through the park, where no one now lingered, no one looking for love or the price of a drink. The flat, when we reached it, was beautifully warm and dim, and sometimes I hated to think of James turning out again and walking all the way back. Once or twice I asked him, tentatively, to stay. Once or twice he hesitated, as if waiting to be persuaded. But it never turned into an issue, and in a way I was glad. I felt that it should not happen like this, although I knew that it might. In my mind I had fixed the childish thought that we must both reach Christmas in this peculiar condition of innocence, of unspoiled expectation, of happy hope. I wanted it all to go properly, to go well. And somehow, in that flat ... I wanted him to take me away. I wanted an hotel, near a lake, in the mountains, where nobody knew us. I wanted us to be alone. I even wanted to wait until he suggested it.

So that in the meantime I took every pleasure that the unresolved situation offered. I enjoyed my friendship with the Frasers so much more that I was no longer officially regarded as subtly unfortunate, although Alix still occasionally referred to me as Little Orphan Fanny. I enjoyed being there with James. And, of course, I enjoyed James. It seemed to me that enjoyment could only increase if things went on as they were for a little longer. After that I would do whatever was demanded of me.

One evening, as we were preparing to leave the restaurant, Alix said, 'This is ridiculous.' Nick joined in, 'No, honestly, nobody in their right mind stays out in the cold the way you two do. You must be mad.' Alix went on, 'What makes you think they stay out? I never believed that for a moment.' There was an odd little pause. It seemed to be up to me to do or say something, but I somehow could not decide what it was. Moreover, I did not see why the decision had to be made in that context, at that point. So I merely laughed, and said, 'Alix, you simply must not tease', which fell a bit flat. She looked at me and said, 'I honestly think you're round the bend,' and, turning to James, 'As for you, I'd be a bit worried by now if I were in her position.' He stared at her, and I thought he was going to lose his temper, but he never does, so he didn't. It passed off somehow. We felt, James and I, strangely apologetic. We felt that they were disappointed with us, irritated by us. We felt that we had bored them, or, rather, not diverted them in some essential way. So that when they insisted on driving us home that same evening, we looked at each other and then said we'd be awfully grateful. It *was* rather cold. Alix insisted on their dropping me off first. She sat in the back of the car, her fur coat wrapped tightly around her, and I remembered how difficult she found the winter. Again I felt a pang for her, and did not mind when she snuggled up to James, who was also sitting in the back. I sat with Nick in the front, ready to be dropped first. I did not ask them in because I knew that the noise of four people would alarm Nancy. I kissed James hurriedly and watched him climb back in the car, next to Alix. And then I watched them drive off. It seemed extraordinary to be alone, for the first time in nearly three weeks.

Alix telephoned me the following morning. She sounded much more lighthearted than of late, and did not even complain of the cold. 'When shall I see you?' I asked, aware that Dr Leventhal had come into the room behind me. 'Oh, as soon as possible,' she replied. 'It will all be much easier now.' 'Easier?' I asked. 'How?' 'Well,' she said, 'more convenient anyway. I've managed to persuade James to take the spare room. That way we can all spend more time together.'

S E V E N

I worried that James might no longer want to see me home, but in that I was wrong. Everything went on just as before. Everything, that is, as far as I was concerned.

In fact it was better. We were always four at dinner, or sometimes five, when Maria joined us, but James seemed more anxious to be alone with me, and we began to leave earlier than before, and sometimes lingered by the Serpentine in that frosty park, before striding on towards Marble Arch and the Edgware Road, and my home. I began to wish that I had asked James to live with us, for Nancy would have made him very comfortable. I had not realized how difficult he found it living at home with his mother, and I felt vaguely guilty, vaguely at fault, for not thinking about him in that protective way that Alix had. Their spare room was very small, and I did not see how he could get all his large austere clothes into that tiny cupboard, but I supposed he could always go back to Markham Street for his laundry or for a change of suit. And I supposed that it was more fun for him, being with the Frasers. I remembered how I had once looked forward to living with them myself, and had so nearly moved in for good. It was only the writing that had stopped me. And then James, of course.

I think he began to love me properly then. He smiled less, looked at me almost angrily, never wanted to leave. Once, I insisted that he stay, something I would never have done had I not felt that change was in the air. 'Better not,' he said. 'They always wait up for me. The flat's so small that they hear me come in anyway. It disturbs them.' This seemed so stupid that I told him that he might just as well have stayed with his mother. 'Well,' he said, 'she waited until the morning to tell me off. At least Alix gets it off her chest straight away.' It occurred to me to wonder why such a strong, severe man let himself be bossed around so much, by women who could not, when you came down to it, claim his attention with as much right as I did. Knowing that I had this right, I never abused it. I did not want to be the sort of futile woman who complains, in public, over trivialities. I wanted him to feel free. And so, when his timing became a little erratic, when he sometimes failed to get to the Library as early in the mornings as he had formerly done, when I sometimes missed him alto-gether, I said nothing. I smiled when I next saw him, and said nothing. I see no virtue in making a man feel guilty. Although I believe it sometimes works.

I began to miss him in the mornings. My exuberant walk to the Library became overlaid with anxiety as to whether I should see him or not. I imagined the three of them having breakfast together, half dressed, in the sort of delightful squalor that I have never been able to manage. I could quite see that he might not want to break away from this new and exciting intimacy in order to drink coffee from a Mickey Mouse mug with someone whom he would probably see later that evening anyway. So strong was my sense that he was enjoying his life with Nick and Alix that I had an image of them, which

101

was worrying on two counts. In the first place I thought I had done with these projections of mine, which never did me any good. I had been living in the present and I liked it there. In the second place, the image, coming from some basement area of my personality and imagination, presented itself as extremely disturbing. Collusive. I saw the three of them talking together, laughing. I was particularly alarmed by this, the laughter. I could find no clue to it.

As if to chase this image, which kept recurring, I walked more briskly, performed my duties in the Library more energetically than ever. I made preparations for Christmas quite as optimistically as I would have wished to see myself doing. If I did not meet James in the morning, I dismissed my disappointment as trivial, as indeed it was, for I should surely see him that evening. What was a little sad was that the pattern had shifted slightly. I still made my way across the park to Chelsea in the cold dusk, but it was now to find Nick and Alix and James all together in the warmth and already deep in conversation when I got there. Sometimes I would not catch up with their allusions until halfway through the evening, and I would not entirely relax until James and I were on our own, although this was sometimes so late that my spirits were a little subdued by fatigue. Even then I found that I could not always match my mood to his. He seemed to be somehow ahead of me, more cheerful, smiling when he remembered something, and saying, 'No, it's nothing', when I asked him about it. I schooled myself not to feel excluded, although sometimes on his face I saw a secret, almost savage, grin which alarmed me. It alarmed me because it seemed to have nothing to do with me. And because I had no idea what could have brought it about.

Fortunately I am very strong and my looks never alter, so that James did not notice anything. But occasionally I felt weary and longed for our earlier instinctive simplicity. I longed, too, for us to know some sort of comfort, for all these arrangements suddenly began to seem to me makeshift, transitory. I began to see why Nick and Alix made fun of our long walks together, why they thought us so childish. It seemed to have been turned into a joke which everybody found amusing but myself. Alix, of course, could only see it as a joke, and Nick, who was not much interested, would occasionally cast his eyes heavenwards in dismay. I suppose it had its ludicrous aspect, but I found that I could no longer get it in perspective. What preoccupied me was the fact that I could no longer *describe* it. Having dismissed the merciless interrogator, the note-taker, that I once had been, I seemed to have precluded the possibility that I might quite simply have told James that I was not happy. Quite literally, I had no voice in the matter. And at times like these I would look at those laughing faces and try very hard to join in. I laughed my way across whole chasms of dismay.

When I looked at James I saw some of the same anxiety. He was not as happy as he had been; I could see that. But our gazes were more serious now; we each measured the other's discomfort. Because we were so like-minded, with grave, correct, and expectant ghosts in the background, we felt surrounded by an atmosphere of bad behaviour from which we could not disengage ourselves and which had its perverse attractions. 'Surely, you must be awfully uncomfortable in that room?' I once asked him, but he only laughed and said that he enjoyed camping out for a bit. It was a change from his mother's spare bedroom, which was pink and white and made him feel like King Kong. And, he added, the Frasers were so enormously entertaining. He laughed reminiscently as he said this. I could understand him, because after all I had experienced the same

103

sort of violent attachment myself. There was no earthly reason for me to grudge that excitement and pleasure to James. Their sort of life was a new experience for him, probably as liberating for him as it had been for me, and I must simply let him enjoy it. There was no reason why it should impinge on our own quieter, but deeper, pleasures.

It was a point of honour with me not to ask him what they said when they were together, without me. I could never, ever, contemplate asking him what they did, for with that odd image in my memory I could never believe that my question would be entirely innocent. I learned not to notice certain things, how he would stifle a yawn, how he would linger with Nick and Alix when I had already left them and walked to the door of the restaurant, how his hair was longer, how his handkerchiefs were now never so spotless as they had been when he lived at home, and how he did not seem to mind all these changes. I learned not to notice his occasional roughness with me when we said goodnight, or his opaque look when I took his hands and said, 'Try to be early tomorrow morning.' I learned not to notice his bad moods, which had never been there for me to notice before, and I thought that maybe he was not getting enough sleep, that he needed a holiday, that I needed one too. And I mentioned this to him, and he turned to me with a look of expectation on his face, of pleasure, and, I thought, of hope, and it was then that I decided that I must get us away somehow, just the two of us. And the plans for Christmas became unimportant and insignificant, as I began to think ahead to the holiday we would take immediately afterwards.

So with this plan in my head I became calmer, and so did he, and although it refused to be anything but nebulous, it was also symbolic and it united us again. 'Don't say anything about it yet,' I told him, and he

104

nodded agreement. This curious need for secrecy was a further bond, but it also altered our plans. We could do nothing elaborate, requiring tickets or visas or hotel bookings, for all of this could easily become public – telephone calls overheard, checking of timetables, arrangements how and when to meet – and it was essential to both of us to pretend that nothing unusual was afoot and to slip away all unnoticed while others were yawning or complaining of boredom or resolving to go on a diet or whatever people do after Christmas. We would go where no mocking remarks would reach us, away from that heightened and hectic atmosphere, so censorious of our innocence.

So I asked Olivia if her family were going to be using their house in Kent over the holidays. She has always told me that I could stay there whenever I wanted to. In fact I know the house well, for I usually spend summer weekends there with the Benedicts. It seemed strange to be asking Olivia if I could go there with James. That is how she came to know about us. I could not tell Olivia a lie.

She looked at me and said, 'Is it what you want?'

I looked back at her, and because I could never tell Olivia a lie, I said, 'I don't know.'

My state of doubt was curious. I knew that James loved me and yet I felt that he was in danger. Or that I was in danger. This was not quite clear to me. I felt that I was being hurried along a path that I had not originally wanted to take, or at least not with so much dispatch, so much secrecy. I had wanted the company of my friends to sustain my golden enjoyment and my new future, but those friends had turned into spectators, demanding their money's worth, urging their right to be entertained. And I no longer wanted to be available for that particular function.

I may have been presumptuous but it seemed to me

105

that unless we were to differentiate between love and friendship we were going to run into all sorts of difficulties. It irked me that I was still supposed to give a full account of my movements and motives to Alix and Nick, whose avid interest, so much welcomed by me in the earlier weeks of our acquaintance, now began to appear in the light of an obligation I might not wish to fulfil. I had no experience of this sort of friendship, although I had observed that it was habitual with Alix: Nick, somehow, was always less involved, leaving the emotional complexities to his wife, who claimed the greater expertise in the matter. Indeed, it was this claim, this expertise, that made her so proprietorial. I did not see how I was to indicate to her that some of her comments were too exaggerated, her questions too provocative, or that in any case I might not wish to answer them. I did not know how to disengage myself from the intimacies that I had found so welcome when she proposed to take me in hand. I assumed, unrealistically, I suppose, that she would view the mature product I had suddenly become and treat it accordingly.

I could of course see that she might be attracted to James, but I dismissed the possibility of this becoming a serious problem. Alix was, as she constantly told us, totally fulfilled in her marriage, and in any case I did not see how she could expect me to defer to her on this point. It was also probable that she was attracted by James's innocence, by the piquancy of a masculinity that had not been squandered. But I, who knew the depths of that innocence, and also its strength when it was shared, doubted her ability to break a bond which in fact she could not understand. It was her genuine bewilderment at our blamelessness that caused her to ask so many questions. And when deprived of answers, she had decided, quite logically, to resort to closer methods of observation. Yet I knew that our simplicity would always escape her. I knew that James and I had recognized this quality in each other, that it was our common knowledge, and that, so long as it remained so, we were safe.

I was perplexed but by no means in despair. If I wanted additional proof of James's love for me, this was provided by Alix.

It was about this time that Alix started to telephone me at the Library, a highly inconvenient move for me because I did not have a telephone of my own and had to trail into Dr Leventhal's office and stand before his desk like a penitent while he waited with massive but pointed politeness for me to go away again. At first the calls were quite inconsequential. How was I? She was feeling particularly dreary, particularly chilled. The winter seemed endless and she was fed up with the flat. She didn't feel much like going out that evening; did I mind if we put off our dinner until Friday? As I had already decided to give no hint of my own distress I replied calmly that, of course, that would be perfectly all right and that I would see her on Friday. I was encouraged to do this by the sound of her voice, which was unusually flat and toneless. It was then that I realized that Alix was not happy.

We were very busy in the Library round about that time, so that I did not have too much time to think. Everybody seemed to have a cold or 'flu, and although Olivia and I remained stalwart at our desks, our task was not lightened by the fact that Dr Leventhal insisted on coming to work, although he had a high temperature and was unable to do much, so that we had to do a great deal more. Mrs Halloran, her face periodically empurpled by a hacking cough, took rather more sustenance at lunchtime than was good for her or indeed for the Library, and would come back at three o'clock quite unfit for further study, although she was still able to cover sheets of paper with her dashing royal blue handwriting.

107

These sheets of paper tended to get swept off the table by the energetic movements of her batwing sleeves; she would then lower herself to the floor to retrieve them, and on one occasion had difficulty in getting up again. Fortunately Dr Simek was not there, and I helped her to her feet, and, at a nod from Olivia, made her a cup of very strong coffee in one of our mugs. 'Thanks, darling,' she said loudly. 'I'm not quite the thing today. This bug, you know. There's a lot of it going around.'

'Perhaps you should go home early,' suggested Olivia. 'You look a little tired.'

'All right, all right, Miss Benedict. I know when I'm tired, thank you very much. Impudence. Nobody tells *me* whether I'm tired or not. I know you want to get rid of me,' she shouted. 'I've got eyes in my head, you know.'

'Mrs Halloran,' I said, 'nobody wants to get rid of you. But you must make less noise.'

'God Almighty,' she said, but rather more quietly. 'Am I bored. Are you bored, Miss Benedict? Are you bored, Miss Hinton? No, you wouldn't be, I suppose. Plenty to keep *you* on your toes, isn't there?'

I made no answer to this, although I saw the light of desperation dawning in her eye, and she might have gone on, had not Dr Leventhal appeared wearily in the doorway and said, 'Telephone, Miss Hinton.'

I went into his room and picked up the telephone and it was Alix.

'Just checking,' she said. 'I don't seem to have seen you for ages. What's going on?'

'It's a bit difficult just now,' I replied. 'Can I ring you when I get home? We're frightfully busy, and I can't talk at the moment.'

There was a pause, and I could hear her drawing on her cigarette.

'You know, you've changed,' she said. 'What's happened to you? You used to be more amusing. More forthcoming. I feel there's a barrier these days. You say one thing, and you mean another.' She paused again. 'Deceitful, really,' she pronounced.

'Alix,' I said slowly, 'there's nothing like that. There's nothing to tell.'

She went on, in a very reasonable tone of voice, 'Well, if that's the way you want it. But it's a bit disappointing, Fanny. I had hopes of you. I thought you might really turn into something. And this business with James ... Well, it's not really fair on him, is it? You think of yourself a bit too much, you know.'

There was a little silence, and a slow exhalation of smoke, and she murmured, '... dragging it out like this.'

I made no answer to this, although I wondered if she was right. Dr Leventhal was clearly waiting for me to go away and get on with my work, but all I could think of saying was, 'Let me ring you back when I get home.'

'Do you love him?' she asked me suddenly.

Instinct, wariness, caution, or all three, dictated my reply.

'No,' I said.

For I think that this was the truth. My confidence that my pleasure would increase and become love had been checked. The easy future that I had imagined had somehow disappeared, and been replaced by the need to be complicated, slightly underhand, pretending that all was well, pretending it to James, and, in a slightly different version, pretending it to Alix. I should not, I felt, have been put in this position. I should have been defended. James should have defended me. And then I thought that she was perhaps right, that I had not considered him sufficiently in the matter. I did not quite know what he wanted. I was not sufficiently experienced to guess. There was, perhaps, a miscalculation in my hopes. I would revise the position after our holiday

109

together, and then I would be able to tell Alix. Who must not, however, know about the holiday until after we were safely together in Kent.

When I walked back, slowly, into the Library, I saw Olivia's eyes on me, a little sorrowful, and I smiled reassuringly at her and went back to work.

That afternoon Alix telephoned again, and this time she was much more cheerful.

'The thing is,' she announced, without preamble, 'Jack and Barbara have invited us to lunch on Sunday, and I thought the four of us might go down in the car. It's somewhere near Bray. We might as well go; it'll save cooking. And I could do with a break.'

'I was going to the Benedicts',' I murmured, wretchedly aware that Olivia could hear me.

'Oh, come on, Fanny. You can get away for once in a while. Don't be such a bore. It's frightfully ungracious.' Quite suddenly she was antagonistic, which frightened me, and I felt it necessary to placate her.

'Of course I'll come,' I said.

'That's better,' she replied. 'Why don't you come round to us about elevenish? That way James can have a lie-in. His poor feet must be worn out.'

'Well, we can fix things on Friday,' I said. 'I don't know what James ...'

'Friday? Oh, Friday. Well, I'm not too sure about Friday, actually. Nick might be working late. I'll give you a ring.'

That evening James took me out for a meal, just the two of us, and my fears were allayed when he walked me home, although it was not our usual walk. And there was no tray of coffee, because Nancy had not expected us home so early, and was still in the kitchen, watching television. We, or rather James, told her not to bother because he would have to leave straight away. I said, 'Are you going to walk back?' and he laughed, and answered, 'Not tonight.' I felt a pang of sadness that the old routine had been so lightly abandoned and then reproached myself because I seemed to be attaching so much importance to outward forms. He took my face in his hands, perhaps seeing my expression change, and said, 'Don't be sad, Frances. Sweet, serious Frances. My dear good girl,' and that made me a little happier because then I knew that he was not blaming me for anything. But I did not like going to bed so unusually early, and I did not sleep well.

The next day, at the Library, when the telephone rang, I found myself stiffening with alarm, and then perceptibly relaxing when Dr Leventhal failed to materialize in the doorway. My remission, however, was short-lived, because in a few minutes he came through the door and said, 'Frances, a word with you, please.'

I followed him out, thinking with dread of that time when Nancy had telephoned to tell me to come home, that she thought I ought to call the doctor. My heart was beating so hard that when he said, 'I have had a call from Dr Simek,' I nearly collapsed with thankfulness, as if I expected the time to start running backwards and all my hard-won assurance to desert me. I could hardly hear what Dr Leventhal was saying, and he looked at me closely.

'Are you quite well, Frances? There's a lot of this 'flu going about, you know.'

I said that I was quite well, although I felt a little off-balance.

'As I was saying, I have had a call from Dr Simek. He is quite poorly, I'm afraid. The 'flu, you know, and now his doctor has advised a rest. But he left some notes here and he wondered if you would take them round to him this evening. He seems to think you know what he wants. Take a taxi, of course. I will repay you from petty cash.'

I was exasperated with Dr Simek, with the fact that

111

I was never to escape from performing this sort of dreary service. In the taxi my mind seethed with images of pleasure from which I was excluded: warmth, intimacy, company, shared meals. I had not been doing anything that evening, so that this did not really inconvenience me. I was simply in a state of tension from which there seemed to be no release.

Dr Simek lived in a large, dull house, up a few worn steps, somewhere near the World's End. The door was opened on to steamy light and a smell of cooking by a woman in an apron, whose face I could not see. I told her my name and why I had come. 'Ah, yes,' she said, in a rather surprisingly cultured foreign accent. 'He worries about his work. I will take you up.' She motioned towards a staircase carpeted with faded red. 'If you would be so kind ...' That was obviously the origin of the phrase. I asked her to go ahead of me, which she did. She knocked on the door of a room on the second floor.

'Dr Simek,' she murmured, and then, in a louder tone, 'Dr Simek. A lady to see you.'

The door opened and a hoarse voice said, 'Thank you, Mrs Lazowska. Most kind.' The landlady, or whatever she was, smiled at me, and nodded her head. I found myself nodding back, and then I went in.

It became clear to me at a glance that Dr Simek was quite ill. He was seated by an ancient gas fire with a saucer of dusty water in front of it, and he was wearing an old silk dressing gown, with a silk scarf tucked into the neck. The room was lit by a bright centre light and contained a narrow divan bed, a chest of drawers with china handles, such as might have come out of a housemaid's attic, a bookcase with a brick under one side, where the leg had come off, and a little table, on which stood a radio tuned to some foreign station. On the back of the door hung one of those awful plastic wardrobes, containing Dr Simek's overcoat and his suit. He himself was seated in a chair covered in rubbed and fading velvet; he made as if to get up, but I went over to him, and put my hand on his shoulder, and he brought the other hand up and patted mine, and smiled.

I had thought I should find him in low spirits, but he seemed to have recovered a certain worldliness, a certain sophistication. When I handed over his file of notes, he inclined his head and murmured, 'Most kind', and nodded to me to put them on the table. I asked him how he was, and he made a little face, and said, 'As you see, Miss Frances. As you see', and then, perhaps because he felt that he had been asking for sympathy, he fitted a yellow cigarette into his old-fashioned cigarette holder, and asked me to sit down. I sat on the bed, because there was nowhere else to sit, and there was another knock on the door, and it opened to reveal Mrs Lazowska, with two tall glasses of lemon tea on a tray. 'Your tea, doctor,' she said. 'And for your guest.' She put a small plate of strange biscuits on the table, and urged, 'Eat, please. Please.' Dr Simek inclined his head to her, as if dismissing her, and she took this as her cue to go.

It was very quiet, except for the roar of the gas fire, and very hot. The tea was scalding, but I drank it as quickly as I could. I was anxious to get out of there, and yet constrained by some old politeness, as if I were a child again, on my honour to behave well. Dr Simek took a lump of sugar in slightly trembling fingers, inserted it between his strong old teeth, and took a draught of tea. The gesture, which was repeated several times, made him seem incredibly foreign, and reminded me, perhaps in the way his lip lifted, that he had been a vigorous man, and, from the way his landlady treated him, an important one. He seemed in no sense apologetic about his surroundings or his dressing gown, and I felt young and slightly awkward. Searching for something to say, I looked round the room and my eye fell on a

113

photograph of a very beautiful woman, on his chest of drawers.

'Is that your wife?' I asked, aware that this was a crude question.

'My daughter,' he replied. 'Zdenka.'

'She is very beautiful,' I said.

'Yes,' he said. 'She was beautiful.' And the fingers trembled a little more, and the glass of tea was raised, and emptied, and lowered again. Then another yellow cigarette was inserted into the holder, and it was quite clear that Dr Simek was ready for me to leave.

'I hope you will be better soon,' I said lamely. 'We have missed you at the Library.' And he gave a fine ironic smile, as if he knew how little difference his presence or his absence made. I stood up, for suddenly this had become unbearable, and held out my hand. He laid his cigarette holder aside, and tried to get up, but found the effort too much. His face sagged as he fell back, and I went over to help him, but with great and unexpected strength he pushed on his arms and stood up, steadied himself with his hand on the back of the chair, retrieved his cigarette holder, composed his face into an expression of worldly good humour suitable to leave-taking, and inclined his head in farewell. He did not, perhaps could not, shake my hand, but remained braced against the back of his chair, his other hand gripping the amber holder.

This image was so powerful, and so disturbing, that when I got home I wrote it down.

And it haunted and irritated me so much that I was longing to see my friends and more than ready for my outing on Sunday. I made an effort and pushed all my doubts and suspicions to the back of my mind, and we had the most wonderful time. We raced out to Bray in the car, James and I sitting in the back, and when James took my hand I looked at him and he looked back and I knew that everything was all right again. It was a fine, sunny day, too good to be indoors, as Alix said, and we decided to cut the lunch and just drive on.

'Barbara always was a bit of a bore, anyway,' Alix decided, waving away our objections. 'I can tell her we lost our way. And then when we really have nothing better to do we can start all over again.'

We had lunch in a pub by the river, and Alix and Nick decided that we ought to have a walk. They went off together arm in arm, gazing into each other's eyes, and James and I looked at each other again and smiled. Then we went off on our own, but we just walked round the garden. The weather had turned warmer, as if spring were already on the way, and we were able to sit down together on a bench and watch the river.

Later that afternoon Nick insisted on taking our photographs. I took theirs, and I don't know whether they came out or not. Then Nick took mine. I found it on my desk two days later. It shows me sitting in a garden chair, in my blue woollen shirt and my blue pullover. I look very young, very trusting, very carefree. Very happy. I have it still. It is the only photograph of myself that I possess.

E I G H T

After that lovely day our attention seemed to slacken, our hold on each other to dwindle. There were only ten days to go before Christmas overtook us. We had a little party in the Library, mainly for the benefit of Mrs Halloran. Dr Leventhal poured sherry carefully into rather small glasses, and I handed round some mince pies. It was not a tempestuously joyful occasion, although Mrs Halloran, who had attired herself in green, with much occult pewter jewellery, had a good time, and after four glasses of sherry became rather sentimental and made a few hazy predictions for the New Year. 'All you wish yourselves, girls,' she proclaimed, as she was to do later in the afternoon when I took her a cup of tea, and later than that, when she could finally be persuaded to leave.

Nick came to the party, and James looked in but did not stay. I had not seen Nick for just over a week, since he took our photographs in that garden, and I was surprised to notice a change in him. He was of course charming to Mrs Halloran, whom he teased as usual, and I was impressed that he stayed as long as he did, for there was nothing there to keep him, and his face, when not creased into his usual golden smile, fell into a sort of blankness. This was so unlike him that I wondered if he were ill, although he looked perfectly well. He looked ... ill at ease, at fault, preoccupied. He looked as if his attention were miles away. He looked absent, passive. He refused my mince pies with a brief automatic smile, then lapsed into a sort of reverie, jerking out of it only to flirt with Mrs Halloran. I wondered if anything had happened, and when we were both out of earshot of the others I asked him. He threw up his hands and made a mock grimace of guilt, and said, 'Sorry, sorry. I'm not very sociable, am I?' which did not answer my question. I remembered the gesture rather than the words. After puzzling for some minutes I remembered that it was the sort of gesture he had used to make when he had not read Dr Simek's article. Or invited him to dinner.

This last reflection worried me. It was then that I realized that I was being slowly excluded from the dinners with the Frasers, or rather that was what I imagined. We had not met for a week. It was of course possible that the Christmas rush had caught up with them, although I did not see why this should impinge on their evenings. It did seem to keep James very busy, for he had numerous small nieces and nephews to think about, and I was all ready to help him shop for them, but he was good at shopping, he explained, and it was easy enough for him to go to Harrods. I had bought all my presents, because Christmas no longer seemed important to me; I just wanted to get it over, and to get away to the Benedicts' house, at Plaxtol, with James.

We were not very busy in the Library, which was just as well because Alix kept telephoning me. Sometimes she would say, 'No news. Just keeping up to date,' and I would put the telephone down and feel absurdly disappointed. I found myself anxious for news, for information. But at other times she was far more worrying, and my knowledge that Dr Leventhal was becoming increasingly testy at the length of these calls compounded my feelings of irritation and of fear. She took her time over these calls, which now all had the same theme: that I was inconsiderate, that I simply didn't know how to treat people, that I had been far from polite to herself and to Nick, and that if I was going to carry on like this I ought to stop seeing James.

'But why should I?' I protested, when she first put this to me. 'What harm am I doing him?'

'You're simply standing in his way. He feels committed to you, and you've told me there's no future in it.'

'I've said nothing of the sort . . .'

I could hear her lighting a cigarette and inhaling.

'You said you didn't love him, didn't you?'

'But that doesn't mean I can't see him. I enjoy being with him. I enjoy his company. He enjoys mine.' I found that I was pleading with her, for the right to continue to see James. 'Why does it have to change? We were very happy . . .'

'There you are, you see,' she cried triumphantly. 'You *were* very happy. Or rather *you* were very happy. It's all self with you, isn't it? What about him? Do you think he's happy?'

I said, 'I'll have to go now', because I was so disturbed that I didn't know how to go on. I wondered if I had really made James unhappy, and if so, what I could do about it. I wondered why he had not told me that he was unhappy, although I did remember his face, stern and downcast on too many occasions when we were together, the eyelids severe. His hands no longer touched my face, as they used to do, but stayed clasped in his lap; their astonishing gentleness had disappeared, and they looked angry again, hard and red. But if the terrible truth was that he no longer loved me, why had he not said so? And if he no longer loved me, why were we going away together? And if he no longer loved me, what had changed him?

It was this last intolerable doubt that kept me connected to Alix, who obviously held the key to the whole dilemma. She must have encouraged James to talk to her, as he had not yet done to me; she must know more than I did. The uneasiness of my situation blinded me to the fact that she had no business to meddle in it, and that I would be justified in asking him not to confide in anyone but myself, if indeed he had anything to confide. The last sensible part of my brain told me that the whole thing was a fabrication, that Alix was bored, that she could not resist a situation which seemed to her 'interesting', and that she might indeed simply be using it for distraction, for entertainment. Because I no longer entertained her. I no longer confided in her. I had repaid her attentions with ingratitude. And that if James were confiding in her it was because he was a better guest than I was and knew what was expected of him. Knew what was due to Alix. That he was humouring her.

This particular line of thought led to a truth which was not welcome. If he were humouring her, it was at my expense. And if he were doing this, then he was less than the totally honourable man that I had supposed him to be. But I could not believe this, although I remembered his new severity, which was quite unlike the severity which had marked him before I knew him properly. Before he loved me. Which led me to the other intolerable truth, which was that he had fallen in love with Alix. Or that Alix had fallen in love with him and was trying to estrange us.

When this thought came I found I could not dislodge it and it swirled round and round in my head with full accompaniment of ugly and erotic images. I saw the three of them in some hateful collusion, as I had once pictured them at the breakfast table, laughing. Pictured here enjoying a joke. My madness disposed them in arrangements which I did not know I knew. I heard Mrs Halloran saying once again, 'She has him by the balls', and I acknowledged the power and capricious will of Alix, her mastery, her autonomy, her fearlessness. She who must be obeyed. I saw Nick's abstracted face at our little Christmas party, and I thought I understood it. I saw James being drawn away from me, because I was too dull to keep his interest. I had thought that we were happy in our modest way, with our walks, our coffee. I thought of our impending holiday, and I knew that I could not go through with it if these questions were unresolved.

On an impulse, I seized my purse, went down to the public telephone in the basement, and dialled Alix's number.

'I'd like to talk to you,' I said, 'about what you were saying. About James and me.'

She sounded very weary, very reasonable.

'I'm not sure that there's any point.' I could hear the cigarette being inhaled. 'I've made myself clear. If you don't love him – and you've said you don't – you're duty bound to tell him that you can't go on with it. That's all there is to it.'

'But it isn't,' I protested. 'I have some feelings in the matter, you know. You don't seem to understand that. And that's what I want to talk to you about.'

She sighed. 'Well, then, come round on Sunday. He'll be out then. It's his mother's birthday. Come about four.'

I said, stupidly, 'I can't. I've got to go and see Miss Morpeth. I go once a month and I can't not go just before Christmas.'

'Oh, for Christ's sake,' she exploded. 'That's exactly what I mean. *Your* little habits. *Your* little routine. And you expect him to fit into that.'

'Alix,' I said, steadying my voice, 'this is idiotic. I don't even know what it's all about. We must talk. Can't I come another day? What about Monday evening? I could come to you after work ...'

There was a pause. Then, 'We're joining Maria on Monday. I'd have to ask her. Oh well, why not? Yes, come on Monday.'

I was shaking when I put down the telephone. I felt as if I were about to come up for judgment, at a court which was already prejudiced against me. And I still could not see what I had done that was so wrong. I was, as I saw it, not only blameless but completely harmless. I was not forcing James to do anything that he might not wish to do. In fact I was not forcing him to do anything at all. Perhaps that was what was wrong, I thought. Perhaps he is the sort of man who likes to have things decided for him. Perhaps he is so upright and severe that I must initiate changes. That I must ask him why he hesitates, tell him that it is all right. That I must make him love me.

I have said that I did not love him in the fatal sense. By that I mean that he was not a drug, an obsession, like that time of which I never speak. I did not have to strive for his attention, I did not have to abandon everything when he appeared, I did not have to squander all my resources at a sign from him. In fact, after the debasement of that previous time, I experienced with James a renewal of innocence, and I felt more at home with that innocence than with that cynicism of desire and contempt so strangely mingled that I had previously known. That secrecy, that urgency, that bitterness, that lack of hope ... I had enjoyed the openness of consorting with an eligible man (how prehistoric that sounds!) in full view of others, after those stratagems and those returns in the early hours of the morning, weeping, my coat huddled round me to conceal the clothes so

121

hastily put on and now creased. The concealed pain, the lying morning face. I could not go through that again.

I wanted, you see, to make it all come out right this time. I wanted contentment and peace for myself and for him and I wanted the approbation of others. Perhaps, above all, the approbation of others. I wanted it to go according to plan; I even wanted the small satisfactions of congratulations and good wishes. I wanted to see the smiles on the faces of Mrs Halloran and Dr Simek as they raised glasses to me. I wanted, for once in my life, a celebration. To make up for all the sadness, all the waste and confusion, all the waiting, the sitting in sickrooms, the furtive returns and the lying morning face. I wanted, more than anything, a chance to be simple, once again, as I was meant to be, and as I had been long ago, a long, long time ago.

I wanted an end to shabbiness, to pretence, to anxiety, to dissembling. That last time, the time of which I never speak, had been so unendurable and also so baffling. I had found myself rising, somehow, to expectations which I did not fully understand: grossness, cruelty, deceit. I had been humiliated, and had been enjoyed precisely because I was humiliated. It was all so different from what others had believed of me. I had managed, somehow, to live two lives. But in the end it was the more respectable of those lives that I had inherited. I minded, of course. Oh yes, I minded. But at the same time I knew that whatever people say and whatever they put up with and whatever they get away with, love should be simple. And it is. It is.

Now, once again, it seemed that I must keep spontaneity at bay, must manœuvre and keep watch. I would do what was required of me – although I was by now so confused that I could not quite decide who required it. I trembled to lose James, my spirit failed at the thought of the expertise ranged against me, I prepared to do battle. But my heart was no longer in it.

I ran up the stairs and knocked on his door, something I had never had to do before. He looked surprised to see me, and rather distant, encased in that professional persona of his. When I explained that I wanted to see him that evening, that, please, I must see him that evening, he gave a little smile, shook his head, as if humouring a child, and told me that he would pick me up after the Library closed, at six.

All that day I trembled steadily, close to anger but not quite angry enough. I was tense with anxiety, with despair, for I doubted my ability to inspire love. If, as it seemed, I had become so uninteresting so quickly, how could I put matters right at this late stage? I was not a powerful woman, able to bend others to my will, nor was I particularly malleable, and therefore able to bend to the will of others. I was not distinguished by notable caprices, I was not irresistibly attractive; I was simply well behaved and rather observant – a bad combination. And my tongue, I am told, is sharp. I was certainly extremely reasonable, but that very quality seemed to deprive me of expectation. Why should anyone care to please me, or exert themselves to try, when I made so few demands? I knew this, I had always known it, but now the knowledge seemed to render me doubly ineffective. At one stage during that long day I caught myself literally wringing my hands, and then I knew how seriously I was dismayed.

I could have been different, I think. Once I had great confidence, great cheerfulness; I did not question my purpose or the purpose of others. All that had gone, and I had done my best to replace it. I had become diligent instead of spontaneous; I had become an observer when I saw that I was not to be allowed to participate. I had refused to be pitiable. I had never once said, Look at

123

me. Now, it seemed, I must make one more effort, one more attempt to prove myself viable. And if I succeeded, I might be granted one more opportunity to do it all over again. I did not dare to think what would happen if I failed.

At half-past five I slipped out of the Library and went to wash my hands, which were clammy. I looked at myself in the glass and I saw my neat watchful face, my alarmed eyes, my white lips. From my bag I took a little-used lipstick and made my mouth pink, then rubbed some of the colour into my cheeks. I willed myself to relax and smiled pleasantly at myself in the glass. When I returned to the Library, Olivia said, 'There's a call for you', and her eyes were as wide and alarmed as my own. I went into Dr Leventhal's room and picked up the telephone; it was, of course, Alix, very friendly, with an invitation to dinner for that same evening.

'I can't,' I said. 'James is taking me out.'

'Yes, he rang to tell me. I thought it would be simpler if you came over here, and then we could put you into a taxi and all have an early night.'

'Well, no,' I said carefully, although I was frightened and annoyed. 'I want to talk to him.'

'You can talk to him here,' she said. She sounded not only inexorable but very reasonable. She made it seem as if there could be no point in my not doing as she wished, and that it would save trouble all round if I agreed to do so straight away.

I merely said, 'Not tonight.'

'All right, all right, there's no need to snap at me.'

'I didn't ...'

'Just send him home early, that's all I ask. He looks worn out. You might think of that for a change, when you can spare a minute from your old ladies.'

'I'll see you next Monday,' I said tightly, trying to

control my voice, and waited for her to ring off, which she did, without a further message.

I think it was then that I decided that I was at Alix's mercy, and because this shocked me so much I took a pull at myself and became more realistic. If, as was unquestionably the case, I had incurred Alix's displeasure because of James's attachment to me, then it seemed as if I must renounce him in order to get back into favour. This was so palpably ridiculous that I gave up the idea straight away. I would, I decided, throw in my lot with James, explain the situation to him, make it seem not serious, even rather amusing, and then ask him what he thought about it. I must, above all, clear the air. I was becoming morbid, I told myself.

He put his head round the door just after six, and nodded, and I picked up my bag and went out to join him. Some instinct made me turn round and I saw Olivia looking at me. Our eyes met, and although I had said nothing to her, she smiled sturdily and raised her clenched fist. In her delicacy, she made no move to leave, in case it should be thought that she was observing James and myself.

I could eat very little at the restaurant, although I believe that the food was excellent at this Italian place: James lunches there most days. He did not seem to notice as I cut up the food and pushed it around my plate; he did not even look at me, although he was in good spirits and very talkative. He seemed to be addressing a point somewhere to the right of my head, and although I wanted to pay attention and seem interested I had some difficulty in understanding what he was saying. I blamed my own distraction, but in lucid moments I realized that he was being deliberately inconsequential; he was talking about matters and even about people I did not know and in that way I could not join in. He was defending himself against me. I could

125

make no inroads on his attention although I knew that it was there, warily, waiting for an ambush, and determined to avoid one. My heart beat strongly, uncomfortably, and all at once I was anxious to get out of the restaurant, to get home, to have him to myself. But he was in no hurry, it seemed, and I could not engage his attention. He would not even meet my eyes. Look at me, I wanted to say. Look at me.

At last he asked for the bill and I waited by the door, buttoning up my coat, tugging at the belt in my haste. It had begun to rain, a fine thin drizzle, and the air felt dank, unhealthy. When he joined me I wanted to take his hand, but he was busy with wallets, with pockets; one hand went to his collar and another to his jacket, to pull it down under his coat, and then at last we set off, side by side, out of step, saying nothing. Then we came closer to each other, instinctively, in the ugly night, and after a while my hand stole out and took his, and that was how we reached the flat, silent, but hand in hand again.

There was no sound from the kitchen and I assumed that Nancy had gone to bed early. Our tray was on the kitchen table, and I left it there. I flung off my coat and went into the drawing room; I switched on the fire and the lamps and turned round to find him standing in the middle of the room, deep in thought. I went up to him and put my arms round his waist, round his damp coat, which he was still wearing, and then I laughed and said, 'Darling, you're soaking. Take this off.' He hesitated, and I laughed again, and tugged at the sleeve, until he shrugged his way out of it. I pulled the two stools in front of the fire, but he did not join me. Instead he sat down in my mother's chair and eased his collar away from his neck. He looked wary, distant, and it seemed to be up to me to take that curiously affronted expression off his face. I could not bear his strangeness. So I started talking, as larkily as I could, and I perched on the arm of the chair, and after a time he grinned and pulled me down on to his lap. It occurred to me that one of us was behaving rather oddly and I assumed it to be me. But his silence appalled me. So I went on talking. I stopped eventually, and looked at him, and smiled, and stood up, and took his hand, and led him into my bedroom, and as I collapsed gratefully on to the bed I relaxed and pulled him towards me. I could feel his heart beating; I could feel his hands tearing at my dress. I thought, but it should not be like this, there is no need ... I reached up for him but suddenly he broke free and stood up and said, 'Not with you, Frances. Not with you.' And as I lay there he turned his back on me and walked jerkily over to the bookcase, and stood there with his back to me. After a minute I sat up, and waited for him to turn round, to explain. But he would not, and eventually I got up and went over to him, and asked him what was wrong. I edged round him so that I was facing him, and I said, 'What is it? What is it?' I said, 'What is the matter?', thinking that I had angered him in some way. But he did not answer. And then, I think, I knew that I had lost him long before the evening had ever started.

I looked down at myself, at my creased dress, the collar slightly torn. I looked at him, but he would not meet my eye. I went out of the room and back into the drawing room and stood by the fire. Eventually I heard him come in, but I remained standing, with my back to him. I heard him come towards me, and hesitate, and then I heard him go out, and then I heard the front door close very quietly behind him. After a while, I raised my eyes to that mirror, hanging by its chains over the fire-place, and I saw my white face, the eyes staring, and the mouth swollen and open, the unaccustomed lipstick smeared all over it. Then, very slowly, I bent down and switched off the fire, and the lights, and went to bed.

The next day I worked steadily, much as usual. The Library was quiet. The telephone did not ring, although I found myself waiting for it. I planned to say that I was not well, if anyone called, and that I was going home. I would then go home. I think I hoped that this would happen, and that people would get worried about me. I think I hoped that if I went home James would eventually come and find me, and that in that bedroom I could somehow reconstruct that evening and make it all right, and then we could begin again and be once more what we had been to each other. But the telephone did not ring, and I was left undisturbed.

I hoped that James would come to me at last, if only to explain to me what had happened. It seemed to me that I had simply not understood some difficulty, and that once I did I could laugh and pretend that it did not matter. 'Was it the wrong moment?' I planned to say. 'I was quite worried. I thought I had done something to offend you.' And then he would laugh, almost out of relief that I had understood and was not upset, and then, if I was very careful, we could begin again. I had this all worked out, and I did not even worry that he did not appear that day, or the following day, because I realized that he had had a shock, and that he was annoyed, and that he did not know how to explain. I began to wonder if I should go to him, and make it easier for him that way, but I could not quite bring myself to do that. I knew that it might be necessary, but I kept putting it off. I thought that I might have to force things into the open before the following Monday, when I should see him at the Frasers'. I could not quite trust myself to behave as if nothing had happened.

But as the hours ticked slowly past, it began to seem as if this was what was going to happen. I felt – and there was not a minute of the day when this matter did not occupy my whole attention – that he should be allowed absolute freedom in this matter, that I should not put any pressure on him, that I should simply put him first. I began to wonder if I had ever done this and realized, sadly, that perhaps I had not. My enjoyment of those tiny routines, which, when I now came to think about them, seemed to dwindle into the occupations of a child, or an invalid, had of course misled him. It was evident to me that I should have got to know him better, that I should have sensed in him a complication, a sort of refusal ... But I had not sensed this. I had not even been aware of it. But if cleverer, more adult eyes than mine had perceived this and had tried to protect him, and in so doing had tried to warn me, then in fact Alix was blameless of anything except rather too much mystification. I realized that I would have to tell her eventually, if James did not speak to me of his own accord, and the knowledge filled me with disgust. And yet, as the time crept on, and James did not appear, I slowly became reconciled to the fact that I would have to go to Alix for an explanation, that it would become something no longer confined to the two of us, but once again a matter among the four of us, as it had been in the beginning.

But on no account would I tell her that he had said, 'Not with you, Frances. Not with you.' I heard those words over and over again, and in the end I came to understand that he had found me ... not suitable in that way; that he had looked on me only as a friend, that this was a friendship that must be preserved in its nursery simplicity, with its healthy walks and its cups of coffee. I thought that I had probably mistaken that early excitement, which I had felt in both my mind and my body, but which he had evidently not felt in the same way. This realization left me numb. And I had told him so much: I had asked Olivia for the house at Plaxtol, and I had shown James that I expected him to be there with me, just as if . . . just as if he would want to be. Just as if I meant anything at all to him in that way. I could never own up to this. Although I knew that Alix, and even Nick, would demand a full accounting, I knew that I could never let them know how mistaken I had been.

As the three days that separated me from the weekend slowly passed, and James still did not appear, my expectations fell away and died, and I knew that he would try to bury the incident and pretend that it had not happened, that he might never refer to it, might not even tell Alix and Nick. I perceived that it might be a matter of good manners to let it all drop, and that it was up to me to terminate our arrangement as unobtrusively as possible. On the following Monday I would be bright and entertaining, for now I needed my friends more than ever. I would plead tiredness when it came to going home, and quite naturally hail a taxi, and I would somehow let it be known that it was all over. It was, after all, what they wanted, in their various ways. And I must not be mulish or uncomfortable about this: it was nearly Christmas, and we were going to have to celebrate together. So that I must be very light-hearted. I would tell Olivia that we had decided not to use the house, and I knew that she would not ask me any questions. I would tell her some time. But not yet.

That was how I came to my realization, and I was amazingly calm about it. I slept badly, that was all. When I say badly, I don't mean that I was restless or agitated. Quite the contrary. I fell into a deep death-like sleep that lasted all the way through until the morning, and when I woke up I would feel quite dazed. I would sit up in bed, trying to readjust to the waking day after what seemed like a total absence, and sometimes, even sitting up in bed, I would drift off again, and feel the heaviness pulling me down. Into these curious, almost amnesiac, states, images would enter, although I could not always remember what they were later in the day. They worried at me, commanding me to remember them. And sometimes they would jump into focus. That was how I saw the rosewood cigarette box again, looking very large. It looked large because I was so small; I was running a child's hand over the slightly irregular, slightly imperfect edge. I was repeating the gesture over and over again. I had nothing else to do, because I was a child and I was waiting for the adults to come back from what was so mysteriously keeping them and to allow me once again into their company.

N I N E

By the time I was ready to visit Miss Morpeth I had composed myself into a facsimile of my former self: brisk, amusing, sharp, my round birdlike eyes on the lookout for oddities of behaviour that I might eventually use in that droll novel that, some day, I was going to write. I had not come round to this state of affairs without difficulty. Above all, the thought of reverting to the role of observer rather than participant filled me with dread and sadness. For although I knew that this was an easy card of identity to use in the game of social interchange, I felt it as the seal of death on any more natural hopes I might have entertained. In my role of observer (and I could already see the reviews: 'witty', 'perceptive', etc.), I should have to prepare myself for a good deal of listening. Without comment, of course. I would somehow be on my honour to extract sly morals from everything, to view the world as a human comedy, to identify connections, to unearth motives. To do everything that I could not manage to do in real life, in fact. I, who found it so difficult to shed my beady isolation, must in fact never appear to be lonely. I must be the odd one at every gathering, and in order to hide my sense of shame I must pretend to be taking notes. Where I had once thought to say, Look at me, I must now turn the attention of others away from myself. I, who had once wanted to be recognized for reasons other than the ones I was now reconstructing, must forget that I had ever sought that recognition. No good would come of it.

I set out for Miss Morpeth's flat on that Sunday afternoon in a mixed mood of deep exasperation and unpleasant clear-sightedness. The exasperation was merely the ultimate manifestation of my feeling for, or rather against, Miss Morpeth, and the perpetuation of this ridiculous duty for which I had not volunteered. As one sometimes tries harder with people whom one heartily dislikes, if only in order to hide that dislike from the other person and from oneself, I tried exceptionally hard with Miss Morpeth. I sacrificed one Sunday afternoon a month to her, and I answered the same questions every time I saw her. I heard the same observations about Dr Leventhal's ultimate unreliability and what Miss Morpeth had said to the Director when she had been invited to sit on the board which had appointed him. I ate the same cake, which I did not like; I spent the same amount of time in the same frowsty room in which the windows were never opened. I washed up the same cups and saucers at the same moment of the day and waited while Miss Morpeth put them away; I heard the same bolts and chains being secured, in the same order, before I felt free to decamp and run down the stairs. As against all this strain and endurance on my part, I did not see that Miss Morpeth was making much of an effort. She clearly found me unsatisfactory, both as a librarian and as a human being, and her resentment of the duties she had to perform for my benefit, such as making the tea, showed in the very stiffness of her walk and the jerkiness of her speech. Besides, I felt, it was time she went to

Australia. Somehow I could not bear to go through that particular conversation again.

The unpleasant clear-sightedness of which I spoke came from my determination to make Miss Morpeth – and indeed everyone else – pay for the penalties they exacted from me. If Miss Morpeth was going to bore me stiff, then Miss Morpeth was going to be used as material. I would write Miss Morpeth into my system of things: she would become a 'character', and in due course I would, by virtue of this very process, gain the upper hand. As I tramped through the park, turning a hard, bright stare on the few passers-by, I was busy writing in my head a deadpan but devastating account of getting Miss Morpeth on to the aeroplane for Melbourne, starting with the purchase of the lightweight luggage, the alerting of Nick (of Nick? I had almost forgotten him), the drive to the airport, with conversation verging on the farcical on both sides (at this point I realized that I would have to go along with them), and then what? I would have to arrange for something unexpected to happen to Miss Morpeth. A romance? Difficult to imagine, given the elastic stocking and the sad green skirt. But if she were to meet someone equally unprepossessing, someone, yes, like Dr Leventhal, I thought I could bring off some kind of rapprochement, since I knew them both so well. The fact that they disliked each other so much in real life would give my authorial tone an extra piquancy. Then, I suppose, having brought them together, I could send them out to a sunny if tentative future together in the Antipodes.

At this point my new sourness curdled in my throat and I had to stop and take a deep breath before I could go on. I found that I could not contemplate the union of two people, even in fiction, without the ground threatening to give way beneath me. Were I to think of two living

134

human beings, ideally matched, and were I to catch sight of them, looking at each other with love, I think I should have died of it. I stood there in the park, on a grey Sunday afternoon, and I fought for control as the tears filled my eyes. That world, in which I was to have no part, how it hurt me! How it reminded me! And how great were the dangers to which I was now exposed, since that defection ... But my vision was so blurred that I took a pull at myself and stared steadily through my tears until they disappeared, and remembered that I could, if I so willed it, gain some sort of a position, lending myself to events in order to control them at a later date. It was, in fact, the only tactic left open to me, and I had better start practising it straight away. All in all, I told myself briskly, this visit to Miss Morpeth was an excellent opportunity. And most timely. For on the following evening I was due to dine with the Frasers, and no doubt with James, and my defences were to be impregnable.

So as I stood in the slightly dingy beige and green hallway of Miss Morpeth's block of flats I performed some sort of surgery on myself and eliminated all feelings save those of mockery and judgment. I registered somewhere, but far away in my mind, that this was a terrible and decisive moment, and that I might never again recover my wholeness. But that wholeness now seemed to me so damaged that it was simply a question of safety, of survival, to protect the ruins, much as certain areas of faulty pavement are cordoned off while workmen heat and melt tar for resurfacing. If I could not ordain what went on below the surface, I would see that what was presented to the public gaze was unmarked. I seemed to have to go through this whole cycle of despair and resolution on an average of once every five minutes, and as I fished Miss Morpeth's Christmas present – an expensive silk scarf – out of my bag, I had

135

to will the weakness away yet again. But by the time I rang the bell I was on the look-out once more, and I was prepared to be deadly.

In my harshness the steps that dragged along the corridor to meet me seemed slower than usual, the hands that unlocked the chains and bolts more torpid. There was even a palpable hesitation before the door was opened, as if the springs that animated Miss Morpeth were wearing out. Determined to chronicle her waning energy with all vigour, I composed my expression into one of smiling ease and found myself gazing at a face I had not seen before. It was certainly Miss Morpeth's face, but so antagonistic that I felt a certain confusion, as if my new initiative, made known to no one but myself, had in fact been taken from me and appropriated by someone else. I was so startled by the sight of Miss Morpeth's face, which had been enlivened with two roughly circular dabs of red on the cheekbones and a crooked smear of red on the lips, and which, tilted upwards, bore a look of weary resolution more suitable, I thought, to my own position than to hers, that I said, instinctively, 'Are you all right?'

She said, 'Perfectly all right, thank you, Frances', and relented, or so it seemed to me, and opened the door fully, and motioned me to go in. I heard her padding along behind me, although she was usually in front of me, and as the kettle whistled in the kitchen she left me to see to the tea, and for once I had to go and sit down alone in her pale green sitting room, and to wait for her as a child waits for its tea. At that moment it struck me that that was exactly how Miss Morpeth saw me, as a spoilt child, who takes its ease of movement for granted, and who sulks when bored, and who, when released from a tiresome duty, will run away and play all the more strenuously because its energy has been momentarily checked. As Miss Morpeth wheeled in the trolley,

I rose to help her, but she said, quite curtly, 'There's no need,' and so I sat down again.

That some change had taken place was quite evident, not only from the colour applied haphazardly to Miss Morpeth's face, but from the rough edges to the usually immaculately cut bread and butter and from the fact that the cellophane paper which had wrapped up the Battenberg cake was folded by the side of the plate, waiting to envelop the cake again immediately I had taken my ritual slice. Into an increasingly dense silence I found myself offering items of information for Miss Morpeth's attention. In this way I told her at very great length about the epidemic of 'flu and the toll it had taken at the Library. I told her about Dr Leventhal's cold, about Dr Simek's cold, and about the little party we had had, and how Mrs Halloran had enjoyed it rather too much. There was no reaction from Miss Morpeth. Then I told her that Nick had had an article published in a learned journal, to which she said, 'Have you brought it?' and I had to confess that I had not. After that there was another silence. Rather desperately I told her about my short story, and this was a measure of my disarray, for I had intended her for the same fate as the fictional Dr Leventhal. Predictably, she was not much interested in this either. I think she regarded it as she might have a child starting to show off. I, in my turn, and no doubt perversely, felt as if she were not pulling her weight in the new mode of existence that I had devised for myself.

It was by now quite dark and conversation had come to a dead halt. In desperation, I said, 'I suppose you will be going to Australia shortly after Christmas? You must be longing to get away from this dreary winter. And it must be high summer in Melbourne. I do envy you!'

At this point Miss Morpeth, who had been staring

straight in front of her, brought her head round and said, dully, 'I'm not going.'

'Oh, but why?' I cried. 'You've been looking forward to it for so long. And your niece . . .'

'I can't fly,' she said.

'Oh, but you must,' I urged her. 'Everyone is scared. I am myself. Every time. And anyway, there are pills . . .'

She flapped her hand wearily, in order to shut me up.

'I can't fly because the doctor says my heart won't stand it. I have left it too late.'

These words frightened me, although Miss Morpeth herself was quite composed, having lived alone with this knowledge and this disappointment, in her pale green room, long before I had arrived on my errand of perverted self-interest. I stared at her and I saw that the colour applied so indifferently to her face covered skin that was more greyish-yellow than I had seen it before, that the loose flesh of her throat was more pronounced, and the rope-like blue veins on the backs of her hands darker and more prominent. Then my eyes fell to her ankles, which I saw to be rigid and swollen, and then back to her face, which was drawn. Her eyelids were drooping over her dull eyes; there were purplish marks on her face. Her hand, which was holding the lighter we had given her when she left, was trembling.

'I am so sorry,' I said, slowly. 'I didn't know.'

'Why should you?' She flashed me a look of contempt. 'We never talked about such things. We always talked about the Library. And I tried to be interested, because I knew that was what you came for. You meant to be kind, I know.'

'I had no idea . . .'

'Frankly, Frances, I am sick of the Library. I do not care what Dr Leventhal gets up to. I never cared for the man. And as for Nick . . . Well, he has never been to see

138

me. Nor has his wife. I asked them both to tea more than once, but they were always too busy. Do you imagine I find all this amusing? Ill-mannered people.' She was beginning to shake.

I said, 'Oh, I think they are ...'

'I know what they are,' she said angrily. 'Do you think I don't understand them? I am simply not interesting enough for them to bother about, or that is what they have given me to understand. They look on me as a boring old woman. Nothing to do with them. Nothing,' she repeated, as two tears were suddenly released from the corners of her eyes and fell on to her sand-coloured cardigan.

'I don't care about them,' she went on, her voice grating, 'but I shall never see Angela again,' and her mouth quivered. 'She was the one I wanted to see. The rest of you meant nothing to me. Nothing.' She pulled a handkerchief out of her sleeve and applied it to the corners of her mouth. 'Nothing,' she repeated.

How odd, I reflected, while searching for something to say, that it should be Miss Morpeth of all people to speak the truth about her feelings, while the rest of us, more fortunate, less impeded, never seemed to find the occasion to do so, or perhaps avoided such occasions lest we should hear something too damaging for our self-esteem to bear. I looked at Miss Morpeth, now tearing angrily at the corner of her handkerchief, her mouth making small gobbling movements, and I saw that maybe the instinct to avoid the truth was a healthy one, for if one were to give way to such a display of naked need how could one ever recover any semblance of adulthood? To have the world see one in such a state of disorder seemed to me at that moment so terrible that I began once again to revise my estimate of human behaviour and to see new virtues in civilized dissimulation. One must, at all events, keep up appearances. And as

Miss Morpeth slowly righted herself, and I sat there warily, waiting for it to be safe to leave, I made a vow that I must never draw attention to myself in that way, must never cry my need. Dry-eyed, I wondered how I might divert attention from my emptiness. And at that moment I knew that I must see the Frasers at once, that very evening, for they had the ability to bring these unmanageable emotions down to a level of curiosity, of gratification, that might, even yet, include me.

As Miss Morpeth gave a sigh and tucked her handkerchief away up her sleeve, I stood up, for it was clear that my presence was no longer required, and also that this would be my last visit. Rather shamefaced, I handed over the little parcel containing the scarf that I had bought for her, for I could find no Christmas wishes with which to accompany it. She nodded her head in acknowledgment, then gave a brief and quite mirthless laugh, which rather startled me, but which I understood when she went to the drawer of a tallboy and produced from it a parcel roughly the same shape and consistency as my own and evidently containing the same sort of silk scarf. In our choice of Christmas presents, we had evidently thought of each other in exactly the same way. The thought chilled me to the bone.

I ran down the stairs, to escape the sound of the bolts and chains being secured, and flew out of the fusty hallway into a chilly but dry and slightly hazy night. It was only half-past five, but it felt like bedtime. In my anxiety to reconnect myself with some sort of existence that might allow me a different fate from the one which Miss Morpeth evidently foresaw for me, I stopped a taxi and told the driver to take me to the King's Road.

As I ran up the stairs to the Frasers' flat, I only knew, very imprecisely, that I wanted to be with them, that I wanted their friendship. More than that, I needed their viability, their selfishness – no, that was not it: their self-interest, their appetite; these were natural and desirable qualities, and I must learn to cultivate them. Or, rather, I must learn to acquire them. I must be near these people, I must be like them. They had everything to teach me. And as for James, I must try to be what was acceptable to him. To them. My heart was bursting with all these intentions when I reached their front door.

There was a muffled noise of melodramatic American voices, and when the door was opened it was by Nick, his face quite blank, and his attention still held by whatever he had been watching on television.

'Fanny,' he said, in belated recognition, as his face momentarily cleared. 'Come in. Quickly.'

I sank down on to the sofa, behind Alix and Nick, who had drawn their chairs up to the television. Between them, on a small table, was an extremely large box of chocolates, and their hands dipped into this as if quite detached from their conscious minds. The throbbing American voices were partially obscured for me by the sound of chocolate papers being scrunched and discarded, nuts being bitten into, and the occasional short-hand remark – 'Ginger. Do you want it?' – which signified to me a state of enjoyment I could only contemplate. Between their heads, past their rapidly moving jaws, I could see fragments of a film in black and white. A beautiful woman in a strapless evening dress was saying goodbye to someone on the terrace of a building. Her lover's kiss reached me in a mutilated version as Nick swivelled round, handed me something, and said, 'Almond cluster.' Then, as he swivelled back again, I could see the beautiful woman, obviously heart-broken, running out of the restaurant or hotel or whatever it was and towards a car with a very long bonnet. The chauffeur, dressed in what looked like a field-marshal's uniform, opened the door and then leaned in to wrap the passenger in a fur rug. As the car drove away I could see the beautiful woman's face, mirroring several sorrowful emotions, staring out of the window. This was apparently the end of the film, although I very much wanted to know what happened next.

Nick and Alix stirred like sleepers. Nick switched off the set, switched on the light, and pushed his chair back. Alix said, 'H'm', and lit a cigarette. Both looked bloated with a sort of Sunday lethargy that never seemed to be available to me. Being with them, and watching their repleteness, was the next best thing to being replete myself.

'What was it about?' I asked, cautiously, for they seemed quite silent with emotion. It was curious how they always reacted to the spectacle of rich people in distress.

'Crap, really,' said Nick, clearing his throat.

'How can you say that?' Alix protested. 'She loved him and she gave him up. That's a pretty serious matter in my book. Hello, Fanny. You look cold. Shall we have a cup of coffee? Nick? Put the kettle on, darling.'

In her contemplation of that fictional renunciation that she had just witnessed, Alix seemed quite luminous with understanding, with compassion. I stared at her, wondering what on earth was going on inside her head, what personal feelings and desires were being given their due. What alibi would she have, I wondered. But when I thought back to Miss Morpeth tearing at her handkerchief, with that tiny regressive movement of her fingers, I shuddered inwardly and allowed Alix all the leeway she would have claimed for herself.

As Nick brought in the coffee, I watched him unobtrusively, taking quick oblique glances, wondering how in the world he fitted into this scheme of things. My earlier understanding of him, as an embodiment of that

142

ideal and fearless male principle, roaming the earth, mentally exacting or enacting his *droit de seigneur*, had undergone some sort of modification. Nick now seemed to me to be more passive, his strength subsumed into that of his wife. Certainly his attitude towards my supposed physical innocence had been paternalistic, even voyeuristic, perhaps, exciting enough to add an edge to my more general pleasure at that time, now lost, alas ... His attitude towards James had always been quite calm, as if, having introduced him into the household, brought him into the circle of his friends, he might now take a rest from active intervention and simply watch the results. I had noticed that although he made the greater effort to charm at the beginning of an acquaintance, he was quite content to leave the rest to Alix. After the initial moves had been made, he was almost absent-minded. What his present position was I simply could not comprehend. Perhaps this ideal couple was so superhuman in its arrangements and its understandings that whatever had taken place would have been beyond my comprehension in any event. I envied them. I felt once more my emptiness, my fear, but mentally I saluted them. Simply for doing what they wanted to do. Whatever that was. Whomever they used. I wanted to be like them. When I felt otherwise, I remembered the silk scarf in its Christmas paper, a present from Miss Morpeth, and, pondering the dread significance of our exchange of gifts, I resolved to go forward, no matter what the consequences might be.

But there were to be no consequences today, that was clear. They were both becalmed by the tremendous emotional experience of seeing that woman in her strapless evening dress driving away from the man she loved, and they sipped their coffee almost wordlessly, still contemplating the blank screen. Then Alix said, 'H'm', again, and pushed back her chair.

I tried to put myself into the same mood, or what I imagined would be an acceptable mood.

'Where's James?' I asked brightly. 'Still with his Mama? Poor James.'

'Actually, Honor Anstey is an *extremely* nice woman,' said Alix. '*Extremely* nice. I'm devoted to her. Yes, he's staying there to dinner.'

I felt a pang on hearing that James had introduced his mother to Alix. I had never met her. Yet Alix was already devoted to her, or claimed to be. I contemplated her range of possibilities, and then my own. I felt some old determination returning, although everything that I had learned that day had been discouraging. Perhaps that was what stiffened me. If, as I thought, Alix had had her way – and I shied away from imagining precisely what that was – then why should it not be my turn to have mine? And I thought of the house at Plaxtol, waiting for us.

'Nick!' cried Alix suddenly. 'How could you?' She indicated the box of chocolates, now three-quarters empty and surrounded by screwed-up wrappings. 'How could you let me eat all those horrible fattening things?'

He looked at her and smiled, the smile of the hunter who has also eaten well.

'How could you?' she went on. 'You know I'm trying to lose weight.' She stood up, releasing a few fragments of cellophane, which fell silently from her skirt on to the littered carpet, and placed her hands round her waist. 'I must have put on pounds. How could you, Nick?' She walked over to his chair and gazed down at him. He, his legs splayed, gazed up at her, at her pouting face, her mock anger, and he smiled his lazy smile.

'Nick,' I said timidly, 'I think you ought to give Miss Morpeth a ring. She's not at all well. She can't go to Australia because there's something wrong with her heart. I think she'll be alone at Christmas. She's fed up

144

with me so I can't do anything. Perhaps if you could find time to telephone her?'

'Jesus,' murmured Alix under her breath.

'Darling, darling,' protested Nick, laughing, 'don't worry. I'm not going to ask her round here.'

He stood up and faced me, his arm round Alix's waist. 'All right, Fanny. I'll do something or other. Thanks for bringing the message.'

Clearly, and for the second time that afternoon, this was my cue to leave.

I was confused and disheartened. I moved towards the door, bulky in my coat, for I had not taken it off, and thought of the hands at Alix's waist. 'See you tomorrow, then,' I said, again very brightly. They smiled and said, 'Yes, yes', as if paying no attention. The dinner the following evening had lost all significance for them, for they were deep in their haste to be alone.

As the door shut behind me I stood on the stairs for a minute or two, unwilling to leave. Then the thought that they might find me still there, and that they might think I was listening, sent me rapidly and stealthily down the stairs, as if I were in fact guilty of eavesdropping. It did not occur to me that I was behaving or thinking oddly. All I knew was that the resolution I had felt earlier that afternoon had undergone some sort of fragmentation, and that I was now in a state of disarray so very nearly like an illness that I began to wonder if I would last long enough to bring matters into some sort of resolution. I began to feel as if my very substance were threatened; I felt the strength of other people's wills about to break my own in pieces. Perhaps if I had gone straight home after seeing Miss Morpeth I would have been all right. I would have repaired myself somehow or other; I would have exercised my autonomy again. I might even have started to write that story in which she was to figure with Dr Leventhal. But, as though by instinct, I had flown to seek the antidote for that distressing experience, for this is what people do in real life. Or so I thought. And all I had found was that I was more incapacitated by the spectacle of normal happiness, no, not even that, of normal satisfaction, than by that of loss, of despair, and of acceptance. For there is something repellent in the spectacle of another's naked misery; it does not encourage friendship. One runs away from it.

And yet there is a special loneliness that comes from contemplating the opposite, particularly when it is so carelessly displayed to one. I walked across the park in the darkness, frightened less of the emptiness around me than of the emptiness within. Edgware Road was deserted, except for a few disconsolate Indians at one of the supermarkets. The nurses' uniforms looked spectral in the unfriendly light. I wondered what on earth I was going to do until I went to bed, and then I realized that, if I wanted to, I could go to bed straight away. Certainly that odd heaviness, as of sleep, was already upon me. When I got to the flat I called out to Nancy that I didn't want any supper, took off my coat, and went into my bedroom. It seemed very quiet. After a few minutes I heard the shuffle of Nancy's slippers along the corridor; the door opened, and then I felt her rough shiny little hand on my forehead, as I had so often felt it in my childhood. 'I'm all right, Nan,' I said, as I had always said then. I sensed rather than heard her go away again. I was so tired that I could barely wait to undress. Then I fell into bed and slept.

T E N

What I had forgotten, in my concentration on the evening, was that Monday was the last day that the Library was open before the Christmas break, that it would, in fact, close down at twelve noon, and with it the entire Institute.

The morning was spent doing the filing, which had rather got left on one side. Mrs Halloran fought a losing battle over the piles of material she insisted on keeping around her like an entrenchment, and then, when I took it away from her, reached into her bag and produced a bottle of ginger wine and a packet of chocolate biscuits. Becoming rather animated, she seized our Mickey Mouse mugs, splashed the wine into them, and handed them round. Olivia, to do her credit, drank with an expression of calm enjoyment; one of her unexpected accomplishments is that she can eat and drink anything. I was not so lucky, but I made a great show of sipping and exclaiming with pleasure. I must have rather overdone it, because I found Mrs Halloran's eye fixed on me with an expression of extreme scepticism. After that I could hardly complain that she had left a small mess of crumbs all over a rather revolting engraving of a scene from Molière's *Malade Imaginaire*, which showed a couple of doctors in shovel hats wielding a syringe the size of a Bofors gun.

The major event of the morning was the arrival of Dr Simek with two bunches of anemones, one for Olivia and one for myself. Mrs Halloran was delighted to see him and presented him with the rest of the ginger wine, of which only about an inch remained, poured into a small glass vase which Miss Morpeth had formerly used for holding pencils. Murmuring, 'Most kind', Dr Simek raised the vase in a papery hand, threw back his head, and drained it in one unhesitating movement. He then inclined his head, placed the vase on the table, advanced towards Mrs Halloran, took her hand and kissed it. Not to be outdone, she rose and folded him in her arms, kissed him on both cheeks, and sank back in her chair, tilting the empty bottle, and then, having ascertained that it was indeed empty, tossing it towards the metal wastepaper basket. Alerted by the clang, Dr Leventhal appeared in the doorway, and, sizing up the situation, said, 'I think we can begin to be on our way. We look forward to seeing you both in the New Year.'

'All the best, girls,' cried Mrs Halloran in desolate tones. The fight seemed to have gone out of her with Dr Leventhal's announcement. I imagined Christmas in a small South Kensington hotel: the tiny tree, the paper hats, the microwaved turkey portions, and the enormous takings at the bar. Olivia and I looked at each other and she nodded to me. Reaching into the drawer of my desk I took out the two Metropolitan Museum diaries, which she had sent for and I had wrapped, and gave them to our visitors. Neither, as I could see, would have the slightest use for a diary, but the pictures were nice. Dr Leventhal had already been presented with the most expensive calendar I could find; the reproductions were of Audubon birds, which Olivia said could hardly be faulted, although last year's, which had shown enlargements of John Speed maps, had fallen rather flat. Everyone professed to be delighted: Dr Simek inclined his head, and Mrs Halloran became emotional, which was what we dreaded, although we did not see that she could manage it over a diary. 'All you wish yourselves, girls,' she proclaimed, with renewed ardour, stowing the diary into her raffia bag, which clinked. 'All the best, Joe.' As we assisted her into her cape, it occurred to me to wonder whether she was addressing Dr Simek or Dr Leventhal, both of whom are called Joseph. Dr Leventhal solved this by retreating into his room, leaving Dr Simek to escort Mrs Halloran from the building. 'How about a First Noel, girls?' she shouted from the door. Then, taking Dr Simek's arm, she gave us a lewd wink, and swept him from the room.

It is extraordinary how everyone assumes us to be totally inexperienced. It must be the way we look.

I went home to Bryanston Square with Olivia and stayed to lunch. I had altogether too much time to waste before the evening and was unwilling to waste much of it on my own. As everybody was out, we had beans on toast and a couple of apples; then we took our coffee into their tobacco brown drawing room, where the windows were always kept tightly shut and the curtains smelt of cigars, and sat down, one at each end of the sofa. We were both creatures of habit, and this interruption of our daily routine was not altogether welcome. 'We can do anything we like,' I reminded her. 'We can watch daytime television if we want to.' But in fact we didn't want to. Olivia, who was tired, said she would go to bed and read for an hour or two, and I decided to walk home and try to do the same. Shades of our childhood, when we always had to rest before a party ... I sought her advice on what to wear that evening, and she thought my grey dress with the white collar would be about

149

right. It is a rather prim dress, but it has a small waist and a full skirt, and it does quite suit me. She reminded me that I was to go there on Boxing Day as usual, and asked if I would like David to pick me up in the car. With her habitual delicacy she did not refer to Christmas Day itself, having retained from an earlier conversation the fact that I had other plans. Nor did she refer to the house at Plaxtol, although at some point she would be forced to ask me when I intended to go, so that she could tell the woman in the village who cleaned for them to let me have the spare key.

I did not altogether want to leave her, although I knew that she really wanted to sleep, so I trailed rather reluctantly to the door and prepared to begin my long afternoon alone. It was quiet in their flat and somnolence seemed to be gathering in the darkening air. In fact it is always somnolent in their flat, which is only brought to life by the disruptive presence of Olivia's mother, with her bags and satchels full of minute papers, agenda, and memoranda. She is the sort of woman who never bothers to take her coat off because she always intends to go out again immediately, and she is in the habit of continuing a conversation she has been having with someone else, as if assuming that her husband and children will tune in with the expected responses. She is genuinely bewildered when they declare that they don't know what she is talking about. They love her deeply and tolerate her not at all; she has become used to being told to close the door behind her, or tidy up her things. 'Come on, Ma,' David calls, 'get fell in.' On Sundays, the only day she is at home for lunch, she looks beamingly around for approval, for she has not only taken off her coat, she has tidied her desk, swept the papers from the sofa, and is prepared to listen as well as being listened to. Those Sunday afternoons, which I have occasionally spent with the Benedicts, are a revelation to me of family

150

happiness. They all talk, which always strikes me as faintly amazing, until the heat of the fire and the peace of the afternoon becalms them, and the conversation dwindles to murmurs. I have seen them all sitting together with their books, each taking sustenance from a different story, but most potently together. Olivia's father eventually makes the tea, and after that Olivia's mother gives a sigh of pleasure and sadness, and says, 'I always forget how much I enjoy Sundays. What a lovely day this has been.' Within half an hour they hear her on the telephone to colleagues – long complicated conversations – and the week has already begun.

I love her because once, only once, during those last days, she took my face between her two hands, and said, 'Whatever happens – and it will happen, Frances – you will never be alone as long as we are here.' Then she patted my cheek, seized her briefcase, and sailed off to a meeting. She regarded my presence in their home as entirely normal, and probably wished, as my mother had done, that I would marry David so that I could be there all the time. This was a matter to which I had given little thought, not because I disliked David, who was quiet and like his father, but because there seemed to me to be no urgency about it. I had the comfortable feeling that David would wait for me to make up my mind; there would be no pressure, no official courtship, simply a gentle, eventual enquiry. I had forgotten him recently and I felt a little guilty; he was too sensible a man to be hurt by me, but I should have liked to have contributed something positive to their family at Christmas. It was just that my mind was too full of my recent adventure and its sad and bewildering development to respond to this thought. As I remembered James I sighed a little and knew that I could not make my contribution either this year or even the next. I knew, ineluctably, that I would always want to know what was happening to James, how he was, where he was, what he was doing. If this was love, it had come not when we were together, but had made itself known most officiously when we were apart. And it had shattered my former unity, made me plan and scheme and try to manipulate events, turned me into a watcher, an outsider. Yet I was still intermittently resolved; I still seized on any reason to make a fight for it; I refused to concede defeat. Simply, I wished that it could have come about another way. I would have wished it to be more straightforward. I would have wished there to be no dissimulation, no mystification, no . . . damage. I would have liked to have met James's mother, and for him to have met the Benedicts, at home. I would have liked straightforwardness, spontaneity, approval. Above all, approval, the good wishes of friends. I would have liked to be the daughter of the house once more.

At the door I turned to Olivia and said, 'Are you quite sure the grey dress isn't too plain?' She said that it fitted me perfectly and that I might as well settle for something in which I was comfortable instead of spending the entire afternoon trying on things and discarding them. I nodded, but my smile must have been half-hearted, for at this point she became very decisive and severe. 'Climb every mountain, girls,' she cried, in a passable imitation of Mrs Halloran, 'Dream the impossible dream', after which we looked at each other, and I said, 'That's it, then', and she said, 'Right', and I went off feeling a little relieved.

I walked home, trying to spin out the afternoon. Christmas was in three days' time, on the Thursday, but most people seemed to have stopped work already. I always hated this cessation of work and the empty streets and the desolation of Christmas. I hated the madness of the people in the supermarkets, buying half a dozen loaves of bread, and the aftermath of office parties, with

girls hanging on to each other on the pavements, gig-
gling, and hitching up the straps of their evening san-
dals. I hated men roaring outside pubs; I hated cars
driving away with crates from off-licences; I hated the
shop windows, especially in the Edgware Road, where
extreme cynicism expressed itself in placing a sprig of
mistletoe in the corsage of the same wax nurse, wearing
the same white nylon overall and cap that she had worn
for the last six months, or where identical tired garlands
of coloured bulbs winked on and off in the window of
the Asian take-away and the television rental company.
Above all, I hated the launderette. On Christmas Day
Nancy served a full Christmas dinner, which we ate
together in the dining room. When we had watched the
Queen, it was time for her to go to her room and rest
until much later in the afternoon, when she would join
me for tea and Christmas cake. While she was resting I
would go out for some much needed air, for on that
particular day of the year I found my surroundings
oppressive, and it was on one of those walks, when it
was so quiet that I could hear the sound of my own heels
ringing out on the pavement, that I passed the launderette, and saw inside the steamy window three men and
one woman, quite well-dressed, reduced to spending
their day like this, and finding what company the desperation of others afforded them. I never wanted to see
that again.

We had had only two Christmases alone together,
Nancy and I. One was immediately after my mother
died and we ignored it, both too aware of her bedroom,
the door closed for ever, the bed still stripped, and
eternal emptiness within. Last year we had managed a
little better, and it was really quite peaceful until I went
for that walk. I saw, through lighted windows, all sorts
of noisy jubilation, in which I wished most strenuously
to join, and then, at the end of my walk, I saw that

launderette with its hopeless and respectable inmates. The day was ruined. I could not wait for Nancy to retire to her television, and I even went to my mother's bathroom cabinet and took two of her sleeping pills from the bottle. I did not need them; I simply wanted to kill the day. And then I wanted to get through Boxing Day and get it all over and done with, and after that to get back to work and not ever have to think about Christmas again.

This year, of course, had promised to be different. It was in the late spring of the present year that I had become friendly with the Frasers and eaten so many dinners with them that I had succeeded in breaking out of the straitjacket that Nancy's expectations seemed to impose on me. And after the summer holiday, at Plaxtol, I had returned to the Library and the Frasers together. At the time of the year when Christmas is the next thing to look forward to had begun my knowledge of James. Or perhaps my lack of knowledge.

I wanted this year to be different, I wanted it to be decisive. However nebulous the events of the past two months, and however little I understood them, I wanted a resolution, and a resolution in my favour. And I wanted that friendship back and with it the expectation of more. I wanted it all to come out right; I wanted to see myself in mirrors, in windows, as I had seen myself in the photograph that Nick had taken that day we had all driven down to Bray. I wanted a future for myself that would be totally unlike the past, and I wanted that future to include not only James but Nick and Alix as well. I wanted there to be four of us again, but within that four I wanted the two of us to be regarded as a couple. This did not seem to me to be too much to expect. I had harmed no one; I had not protested. I had not reproached, said anything drastic or irreparable. What had happened, I told myself, was that I had become a little tired and over-sensitive to nuances of

154

behaviour that might not even be intended. But that would change. I had only to take a pull at myself and be tactful and light-hearted (yes, light-hearted; that was essential) and all these misunderstandings would lift like morning mists at the beginning of a perfect day.

Bathed, and neat in my grey dress, I went over to the mirror to see how I looked. I looked ... odd. I looked, in fact, rather chic but rather plain: not a hair out of place (it rarely was), round eyes watchful. My appearance, which I had accepted ever since I decided that I could only get by on style, no longer pleased me. I looked, I thought, like some beady Victorian child. I moved to the cupboard to search for something more interesting to wear and when I glanced back I saw a more flattering side of myself in the glass, a small waist, a long back, a full and flattering skirt. And it was getting late, so I took a deep breath and tried to look more interesting, and willed my face into a softer, less critical expression.

I no longer liked that room, in which things had gone so wrong. I picked up a nail file and smoothed out a rough nail and tried to be rational about it, but I found myself trembling and the nail file skidded. There was, I told myself, no need to stay in that room; there were, after all, three other bedrooms. Nancy pottered in with some clean sheets, and, on an impulse, I said, 'Don't change the bed, Nancy. I think I might move to one of the other rooms. I'll decide tomorrow.' Tomorrow would be a day of decisions. And before she could start worrying about this, I took my coat, kissed her good-night, and left the flat.

In the streets it was office party fall-out time: groups of girls hanging on to each other and collapsing with mirth, flushed young trainee managers banding together to exchange boasts and resist further onslaughts from their secretaries. I threaded my way cautiously between

155

these knots of people, who were straying all over the pavement, and then I was past the main crowds and under Marble Arch, and at last in the park. The weather had turned mild again, as it so often does just before Christmas, and there was rain in the air. It was the sort of weather that encourages one to walk miles, and I wondered if I should be accompanied home, through the park, later that evening. I did not think beyond this, but far away beneath my reserve and my careful monitoring of my expression, there was the most agitated hope.

In the course of this walk, which I knew so well, my thoughts became clearer and less worrying. I decided that whatever had happened – and I still did not know or understand what had happened – I would behave as if everything were normal, regular, above board. I tried to take some comfort from the fact that I had given no indication of hurt, had uttered no words of blame, had made no confession to anyone. I must, I thought, simply hope against hope that the serious business of my life would be proof against those strange events that had appeared to turn it off course. I made all sorts of sensible resolutions: I would be cheerful and good-hearted and straightforward, and if, at any point, I became aware of what I suspected to be mischief, then I would quite naturally question it, ask for an explanation. I had been too subtle, I thought. I had tried to deal with this on my own, without looking to others for the truth. I had judged it a matter of pride to behave as if nothing were amiss. I had probably been insufferably smug; no wonder my friends had thought me tedious and disappointing. I determined to change all that. By the time I had come out into the lights of Knightsbridge, I was smiling, firm in my new resolve.

I knew that I had to be light-hearted, and I brightened my smile before I had even rung the Frasers' doorbell. The door was in fact open. 'In here,' shouted Alix. 'In the bedroom.' Still smiling, I went into the bedroom to find Nick and James in conclave, standing behind Alix, all of them facing the glass of her dressing table. 'I think definitely up,' said James, referring to the perennial question of her hair. As I had bought her some antique tortoiseshell combs for Christmas, I echoed his approval. She, turning her head from side to side, and smoothing the wisps at the back of her neck, arched her back, and said, 'H'm. What do you think, Nick?' I saw that she was wearing a very tight black jersey dress, cut low at the front, and I said, 'Goodness, how smart you look!' But she was still turning her head critically from side to side and there did not seem to be any way of securing anyone's attention until this scrutiny had run its natural course. James and Nick were as grave as if they were discussing a serious case, and their rigid frontality, their three faces staring into the glass, left me peering uncomfortably behind them, addressing their backs. 'You know what I think, darling,' murmured Nick, and after a minute's pause, she suddenly pulled out the pins and released her hair. 'You're right,' she said. 'It never suited me,' and James and I chorused eagerly, 'Oh, but it did.' 'No, no,' she said, brushing and brushing away. 'My husband is always right.' And she smiled up at him and gave her throaty giggle. By that very action she seemed to be alluding to areas of intimacy, while at the same time reaffirming the exclusive bond she had with her husband.

I had always known that Alix had unusual abilities, but I had never seen them in action until this moment. With one tiny concession, on a matter of inconsiderable importance, she had succeeded in annihilating the thought of transgression in our minds and had re-established the image of Nick and herself as the perfect couple. And yet I could see from the way that James was following her with his eyes that in spite of this little performance, or indeed because of it, he still sought her approval. She looked older, more powerful, in her tight black dress; the curves of her figure seemed more opulent than usual, reducing my dwindling confidence still further. Blameless and understated in my grey dress, I could capture no one's eye. Look at me, I urged silently. Look at me.

And indeed it seemed as if there were only the three of them present, and as I followed them down the stairs, I felt, in a curious way, outclassed. I was still smiling brightly, but all to myself; the three of them seemed to move as a unit, all tall, all handsome, physically linked. I did not permit myself any judgment, but I could feel rage and terror gathering, and I had to exert myself to keep these emotions at bay. This made me very silent, but as no one addressed a question or even a remark to me, my silence was not noticed. Or perhaps there was a tacit agreement not to notice me at all. In this way, still smiling, but as alert and wary as an animal, I sat down with them at their favourite table.

Maria was already there, looking equally dressed up in satin trousers and a white ruffled shirt. She sauntered, almost swaggered, through the crowded space, and clapped Alix on the back. 'Wretch!' she shouted. 'You said you'd telephone this afternoon,' and soon they were arguing strenuously about who had said what. I had always found Maria a slight embarrassment: her low hoarse voice and her haughty physical presence had made me feel uneasy in some non-specific way. But she had always been very kind, and if I regarded her perpetual sparring with Alix as a sort of bad manners, I recognized that they shared a boldness which I simply could not match. My appeal, I had thought complacently, when I was happy, was precisely that I never overstepped the bounds, never caused social anxiety. I still thought that, even now.

158

While we ate I found myself trying to place remarks and failing, reduced to exclamations of 'Really!', 'Oh, I'm sure you did'. Even these did not manage to meet their mark. As on that occasion with James, I somehow failed to catch the drift of what was being said. There seemed to be an argument, which was half serious, half joking, between Alix and Maria and the two men looked on enthralled. As all this referred to something that had taken place when I was not there, I could neither join in nor understand what it was about, and my smiling exclamations appeared ridiculous even to myself. I became quite silent. I looked at James and saw that he was enjoying himself; his face was highly coloured, and although he was seated next to me he was half turned away, as if to face Maria. The thought that he could not even bear to look at me was so terrible that it did not occur to me that he was being very impolite. And anyway, what sort of a half-baked, old-fashioned notion was impoliteness in the midst of this avid crowd, their eyes glistening with mockery and pleasure, their extraordinary conversation now so allusive that I felt a touch of nightmare, as if this could not possibly be happening except in a bad dream?

Maria clapped Nick on the back, and said, or rather shouted, 'How do you deal with this bitch?'

'You be nice to me,' Alix countered. 'Everyone has to be nice to me this evening.'

'Why?' I asked, really for something to say.

She sighed dramatically, laid her head on one side, lowered her eyelids, and whispered sadly, 'Because I've come down in the world.'

They collapsed with laughter, and James and Nick chorused, 'She's come *down* in the world', and they both leaned forward and kissed her. Nick kept his arm round her, and she looked at him, her eyes alight. 'Ho, ho,' said Maria. 'Christmas has started. But not here, please,' she

159

cried, flinging out an arm. 'You are embarrassing Fanny.' And they all laughed again. And I, of course, smiled.

At other tables people were turning round, grinning, shaking their heads in amused indulgence at these antics. It was very hot and there was an atmosphere of excitement. Alix lit a cigarette. 'Not yet, not yet,' cried Maria. 'Not before the pudding', at which point a waiter approached our table with a huge, towering concoction largely composed, as far as I could see, of whipped cream. There was a roar of delight, and Maria seized a spoon and doled out large portions on to our plates. The sight of the yellow and white mass gave me a momentary pang of nausea, but the others were exclaiming with delight, and soon the sweet liquefying mixture was being attacked, devoured. 'More, more,' shouted Maria, piling spoonfuls on to my plate, and ignoring my protest. 'More, more', and she bent over James, who was laughing, and said, 'More, darling. I want you to be good and strong tonight. More.'

I stared down at the yellow custard on my plate and willed my shock not to show. And when I raised my head, it was to look calmly and even smilingly at Alix and Nick. Who were, of course, watching me. I said, 'It was delicious but I really couldn't eat any more.' Then I turned my head and looked at Maria, who was flushed and laughing. Then, when I could trust myself, I looked at James. His eyes were fixed on Maria and his face was foolish with desire.

'H'm,' said Alix, who appeared to be slightly cheated of the 'interesting' situation she had foreseen or even contrived: I should never know. I should never refer to it again. I was aware that if I made some sort of a scene, they might have warmed to me in sympathy. The trouble with good manners is that people are persuaded that you are all right, require no protection, are perfectly capable of looking after yourself. And some people take your impassivity as a calculated insult, as Alix seemed to be doing now. Still I smiled.

The faces before me seemed to me to be flushed, venial, corrupt, gorged with sweet food and drink, presaging danger. Smoke wreathed through the hot air, and flakes of ash fell on to the unheeded plates. Alix stubbed out her cigarette in the remains of her yellow custard and smeared red over her wide mouth. Nick encircled her with his arm. I did not dare to look at James. It was very hot, and I knew that I must get out soon, but that I must not betray my haste.

'H'm,' said Alix again. 'I suppose we'd better go.' I took out my purse and, smilingly, insisted on paying the bill. It was, in any case, the last meal I should ever eat here. 'I suppose we'd better leave these two together,' said Alix. Still I smiled.

'What are you doing for Christmas, Fanny?' she asked.

Very calmly, because I was now in such a state of terror that it seemed as if nothing could get worse, I said, 'I suppose I shall go to Olivia.'

'Rather you than me,' she said.

'I don't understand,' I queried, with a polite, upward turn of my head.

'Well . . . can't be much fun, can it?'

'Why?' I asked.

'Well . . . she's crippled.'

I said, 'Only physically', and I must have spoken rather loudly, because there was a brief silence.

After that, it was quite evident that the evening was over. They stirred and put on coats, and although I walked ahead of them to the door it was a matter of pride to behave as if I were still in their company. I did not look back. I simply went out on to the pavement, and, still smiling, and with a brief wave, I walked briskly away from them, down the street.

E L E V E N

And then I was alone, in that emptying street, with the night's blackness to hide me.

I maintained my airy walk and my smile was still on my lips. For as long as I thought that Nick and Alix might take it into their heads to worry about me and offer me a lift home in their car, I sauntered along, looking amused and nonchalant, as if having witnessed some particularly rare episode of the human comedy, available only to connoisseurs of the absurd. My hands in my pockets, my head tilted at its usual enquiring angle, I took my time, perusing articles in shop windows, stepping unconcerned from areas of light to areas of darkness, attentive to the hiss of tyres behind me, waiting for a car to stop and a voice to hail me. I would have gone with them. Yes, even then I would have gone with them. For what I felt, beneath the bright factitious surface of my outward appearance, was an enormous sense of loss. It no longer seemed to me important that I had been duped. I was so tired of not apportioning blame that I could no longer see where it was due. I felt, simply, irradiated by the blast of some great revelation, although I could not yet fully understand the nature of that revelation. I could not, somehow, make contact with any familiar emotion. As I lingered in front of a lighted window, apparently beguiled by a pair of burgundy leather shoes, I could only identify a feeling of exclusion. I felt as if the laws of the universe no longer applied to me, since I was outside the normal frames of reference. A biological nonentity, to be phased out. And somewhere, intruding helplessly and to no avail into my consciousness, the anger of the underdog, plotting bloody revolution, plotting revenge.

As for James, whom I loved all the more for having lost him, and more even than that, for having seen him reveal himself as a true man, with desire in his eyes, a lover at last, well, James, it was simple, James was ... like them. No mischief had been practised, for you cannot stand between a man and his inclination, if that inclination is strong enough. I would have thought, before this evening, that I understood what love was about. Given the chance, I would have laid down my life ... Being of a sacrificial disposition. But clearly, matters have to be taken in hand, attentions redirected, if unsuitably placed. Clearly, for love, a rampant egotism serves one better than an unsophisticated hope. I remembered the noise and the heat of that restaurant, the intent and flushed faces, the oozing custard, the sucking inhalations of cigarettes, the raucous but sly excitement, the watchers. That, clearly, was the correct atmosphere in which love might flourish. And, come to think of it, why not naked competition, black propaganda, ruses, devices, stratagems, insinuations, blackmail, trickery, cruelty, desertion? Why not the triumph of the will? And why be sad about all or any of this? If, as we have it on the highest authority, there is more joy in Heaven over one sinner that repenteth, why not sin, provisionally? Why not break the rules, like that Prodigal Son (so much more amusing than his tedious

163

brother) who must have attended so many parties like this evening's, and who still came home to enjoy the fatted calf? Because they had felt so dull without him. So extremely bored with only the spectacle of virtue and hard work to beguile them.

The noises of the street were becoming fainter, and, to give them a last chance, I lingered outside Harvey Nichols, watching a small electric train racing silently round and round. When I raised my eyes from this, it was to meet my own reflection, small, slight, undeniably chic. Not a hair out of place. Still poised, still terrified, still murderous. A person, you would say, of no overt desires or needs. Well provided for. Decently housed. In extremely good health. A person who had not, in any sense of the word, come down in the world. And who could be relied upon never to cause embarrassment, either of a social or a personal kind. For that very reason, perhaps, rather less than interesting. And quite talented, with two stories already published in a prestigious American magazine. Embarking on a novel, it is said, calculated to be much appreciated in donnish circles. No immediate plans, but then, when one is a writer, one does not have the same plans as other people. One is not expected to. One is, let it be remembered, an observer, an unblinking eye recording what is thought, at the time, to be unremarkable. These scenes, these actions, to be retrieved, at a later date, intact. No blame attaching, of course. Able to see the funny side.

For it is all extremely funny, the misplaced enthusiasm, the expectations. Running like an acolyte to those who did not need me and like a fiancée to one who made his choice elsewhere. And even now, standing in front of Harvey Nichols, watching an electric train race round, my eyes, when I raised them to the darkened glass, were brilliant with tears and spite. It had to be funny. For if one is serious, one is rarely a welcome

164

guest. Everything must be converted, somehow, into entertainment. And I could do it. I might not want to, but who cared about that? I could do it. And when a secret is known to the whole world, no one will ever suspect that it was ever a secret in the first place.

The street was almost silent now, and empty of cars. The rain, which had been threatening all day, making a dark afternoon and a seductively soft evening, now came blowing on the wind, disruptive of one's appearance, unsettling. I took my leave of the train set, crossed the street, and, almost automatically, entered the park. I was in no hurry to get home, although it occurred to me that what I was doing might be rather dangerous. I thought, childishly, that if it had really been dangerous, they would have stopped me. As they had not, I would put myself at risk, just to see.

I was unprepared for the darkness, and the silence. I had never noticed them before, as I had always been hurrying to Chelsea on a visit, or walking back with James, my face turned towards him. On every occasion, my head had been crammed with words. Now, when I needed them, they had deserted me. Vacant, I was sur-rounded by vacancy. It was extremely undramatic. Apart from the fact that my feet stumbled when they encountered soft earth and tripped when they got back on to a hard surface, I was not aware of any sensation whatever. Once past the edge of the Serpentine and the darkened café, once on to the gravel again, I stopped for a moment at that point where one can take one of three paths in the direction of Marble Arch. A clump of broad, squat, leafless trees, perhaps no more than three or four, but dense and compact in outline in this uncertain light, stood sentinel by the side of the main centre walk, the shortest distance to the other side. But I was not anxious to reach the other side, and so I turned to the right and

165

embarked on the narrower path that would lead me in an oblique angle, to where it was darkest.

Emptiness flowed away from me on either side. The rain was now steady but silent, falling in such thin threads that one was aware of it merely as a coldness descending. There was no evidence of life around me, no rustle in the undergrowth, no reassuring country twitterings. The park, at night, was empty of comfort, a place for outlaws, for those who desired concealment. I was entirely alone, and might have gone on like this indefinitely, had I not, too soon, reached the darker avenue of trees which ran parallel to Park Lane. Now I could hear a sizzling sound, as the occasional car seethed along on the wet road. Lights, in the big hotels, merely served to accentuate the opacity in which I moved. There was a moon, revealed and again concealed by drifts of black vapour, but it did not reach down into my darkness and was in any case on the wane.

I found, in a curious way, that I was walking from memory, for I could see nothing ahead of me. I could hear ordinary city sounds, muted by the late hour, to my right, but they seemed to have nothing to do with the cessation of life in the narrow enclave in which I moved. I was at no point afraid, even when I heard footsteps behind me, a soft steady pounding of deadly purpose-fulness. Indeed, I could barely be bothered to turn my head as the silent runner, in shorts and sweatshirt, eventually overtook me, and then I could hear his laboured breathing and smell his sweat. Once he had disappeared, the silence was even more intense. My thin shoes made no sound and my black coat made me at one with the unmoving columns of the trees.

In fact it was so restful, so appropriate, that at one point I sat down on one of the seats, congratulating myself on the extremely controlled way in which I was handling what might, to others, seem an unpromising situation. Still in this mood of tight control, I made plans. Changes would have to come about, I thought practically. I could no longer go on living in that flat, with its two-fold layer of memories. I would pension Nancy off and send her home to her sister in Cork. I would tell her after Christmas, and once she was settled, put the flat on the market. It would bring me in a tidy sum, and with this I would buy an attic, a top floor somewhere, in a different area. I liked the small shopping streets near Victoria Station. I might even give up my job, for I no longer needed the money or the occupation. I would be a writer, my material spread out before me, the whole world my oyster, free to invent my life. I doubted if I should marry David, for something inside me had become fissured by alarm, as if exposed to some violent and deathly ray, resulting in a kind of sterility. I loved his family too much to wish on him a wife unable to understand or to trust affection given naïvely, worthy of good faith. Since leaving the silent train set, emblem of so much Christmas expectation, I had felt myself growing smaller, harder, more brittle, less worthy of love than before. I felt dangerous and endangered. The sooner I cut adrift, the better. I felt I should go where no one could watch me, check on how I was bearing up. I would deal with matters in my own way, far from scrutiny. My own views, so far unsought, might eventually find their way to the light of day.

I had no idea of the time, although it must have been very late. When I felt cold, I got up and resigned myself to walking on. There was still no sign of life. I strolled, in an almost leisurely manner, in the direction of Marble Arch. Far ahead of me, a tiny light, at waist level, wavered, was gone, then reappeared. My coat was damp, my face cold; I could feel minute drops of water on my eyelashes, which made the outlines of the trees hazy. The light came nearer. At no point did I feel either fear or curiosity, and when a policeman, on his bicycle, asked me whether I was all right, I answered, as briskly as I could, that, yes, I was perfectly all right and was on my way home. I often walked this way, I told him, feeling him to be unconvinced. And indeed I quickened my pace, for he had got off his bicycle and stood, watching me, and I could feel his eyes on my back as I went down the steps to the underpass.

In the thin glare of the mauvish lights the endless tunnel stretched before me, a far more frightening sight than the dark and empty park. There was a stink of urine, and someone had recently been active with an aerosol, for several fresh slogans in blue Arabic writing decorated the tiled walls. 'Victory to the Revolutionary Council in Iran', proclaimed a grease pencil, applied to an otherwise innocent poster advertising men's dress suits for hire. There was no one in sight, but now I felt a touch of unease, and my footsteps drummed out rather more loudly, their echo coming back to me. At one point I stumbled and must have kicked an empty lager can, whose mournful clatter, a doleful sound, made my teeth clench and sent me hurrying on. Then, just as I felt the first faint stirrings of alarm, a figure staggered round the corner ahead of me and came to a groaning halt, propping itself against the wall, and bending over as if in an extremity of pain.

Heels drumming, and eyes staring steadily ahead, I walked towards him. I could smell the whisky and hear him mumbling and groaning. Out of the corner of my eye I could see him bending over, as if to vomit, and then righting himself; then I could see him spread-eagled against the wall, one hand, with thick black nails, splayed on the tiles behind him. As I came level with him, the other hand reached out and made as if to grab my sleeve, but his aim was too unsteady and he missed it. This angered him, and his voice came to me, a

168

threatening animal sound. I stamped on, electric with terror, assuming an expression of worldly indifference, as if I had not noticed anything amiss. Only when I had reached the other end of the tunnel and was about to turn towards the steps did I dare to look back. I saw him, propped against the wall, his hand still stretched out, feeling for me. His face was a darkish purple.

By now I was shaken, and I felt my confidence or my madness or whatever it was leave me. I felt the blood drain from my face and the heat from my body; I felt my shoulders contract, and my hands start to tremble. I would have run the rest of the way if I had had the energy, but this seemed to have deserted me. Oxford Street looked like a dull chasm, with ghostly Christmas trees in shop windows illuminated only by those terrible acid overhead lights. I looked at my watch; it was half-past twelve. For some reason the thought of taking a cab never crossed my mind; in any event, nothing passed me. I felt as if I had to accomplish this ritual on foot, and that only if I did so could I face the haven of warmth and muffled air that awaited me. Only in this way could I exhaust myself sufficiently to put thought to sleep, and if I did not so exhaust myself I would feel that I was entering a tomb, rather than a perfectly ordinary bed. As I turned up the Edgware Road, the home stretch, I even thought with longing of the hot drink that Nancy would have left for me, and of the safety of her presence, her protection.

I was not very fast now, and my feet stumbled from time to time. I went past the sex shop, and the television rental company, past the ethnic hairdresser, whose fluorescent tube in the window blinked weakly, lessening my feeling of total desertion. I greeted the wax nurse in her spectral uniform like an old friend. I passed the banks and the supermarkets and mysterious shops which seemed to have an air of dereliction about them and whose normal purposes I could now no longer re-member. The rain had stopped but my coat was damp and it impeded me. I felt intimations of nightmare; I seemed to be making no headway. It was as if I were trying to wade through some viscous substance wearing an old-fashioned diving suit. There was no one in sight. There was no sound, apart from a distant rumble, which I could not identify. I was breathing harshly now and I could feel a pain in my chest; my hair stuck to my damp face in wisps, and I was very thirsty. The dull rumble came nearer, and I was aware of a dark shape looming in front of me, high above. Then I realised that this was the flyover, and that I should have to negotiate another underpass in order to get to the other side, and home.

For some time I could not do it. I clung to the railings and waited to feel better, and still did nothing. I think I even decided that I might stay there until someone came along and then I might summon up the courage to follow them down those steps. I was prepared to wait until the morning, but I was so tired, and it was so dark, that this immediately became unimaginable. Several times I started down the steps, only to retreat to the surface, my mouth dry. I could not go down there. I knew that people sometimes slept rough in subways, that they were the favourite haunt of drunks and dere-licts. I thought of the man at Marble Arch and I smelt the smell again. I think at one point that I must have sat down on the steps and buried my face in my hands. I had never had to do this before, on my own. James, who knew I was frightened, had always put his arm round me, and that way it was even enjoyable. And thus I felt his loss again, and the loss of all protection, and I tried to summon the compensating anger. But at some point on that homeward journey, even the anger had retreated from my grasp.

And then, after about half an hour, I managed to go

down the steps. But I was shaking so much that I had to cling to the railing, feeling for every step with my foot, and then, when I had reached the tunnel, keeping close to the wall, the dirty tiles, ready at the slightest sound to retreat, or, when I had passed the halfway mark, to fling myself forward. It took a long time, that I know; I also know that when I reached the steps at the other end I could hardly lift my feet to climb them. At one point I was overcome with a sort of vertigo and had to stand still until I found the will to go on. I emerged upwards into the blackest night I had ever seen.

This must be the most terrible hour, the hour when people die in hospitals. No sound, no light, the vital forces ebbing away, even the memory indistinct. I had no reliable information on where I had passed the earlier part of that evening, nor could I really understand what had happened, or how I came to be here. I only knew, as I passed dreamlike along the endless empty street, that I must get home; I even put my hand in my bag to get my key, and I held it before me like a talisman as, light-headed, and vague in my movements, I reached the corner where the Westminster Bank stood four-square, as it always had done, and when I lifted my eyes I could see a very dim glow behind the curtains of the drawing room, as if a lamp had been left on for me.

It took me a long time to climb the red-carpeted stairs. I felt like a pilgrim who at last reaches the place of his pilgrimage, after days and nights of search and exhaustion. I noticed, as if it were some item of sacred furniture, the gleaming brass of the stair-rods; my hand crept out and touched the wooden banisters. Slowly I looked around me. I had reached the end of my journey. I raised my hand and with it the key.

The door was locked. Nancy had locked the door.

After a time, or rather a complete absence of time, I rang the bell. Then I rang it again, aware that I was

171

doing something so untoward that it had never happened in this house before. This place of regularity, and sound, if valetudinarian, habits, this serious place, always so quiet and so measured, was now violated, at two in the morning, by the harsh sound of a peremptory bell. I imagined people stirring with alarm, with outrage, as their night was shattered. I expected to see the ranks of the elderly, in substantial dressing gowns, in solid slippers, massing at their front doors, ready with admonishment, shaking their heads. I awaited complaints. I stared around me, as if on trial. Then, after a long silence, I heard the soft shuffle of Nancy's steps, and the chain sliding, and the latch going up, and at last the door was opened and I was staring down into Nancy's severe and trusting blue eyes.

I must have looked very odd for she said nothing, merely put out her hand and laid it on my sleeve. As I went forward, but so slowly now, she took my arm in both her hands, and then I felt her arm around me, and, quite wordlessly, we walked along the passage. She guided me into the kitchen, and put on the light, and as I sank down into her own padded basket chair, she shuffled over to the cooker and got busy with the kettle. I was still wearing my wet coat and my feet were swollen; my eyes seemed to me to be shuttered by my drooping lids, although Nancy tells me that they were wide and staring. As she made the tea, my ears adjusted to this new form of silence: I heard a singing in the pipes, the occasional jerk of the hands of the kitchen clock, the bubbling of the boiling water poured into the teapot. Then I felt the cup guided towards my mouth and I drank steadily as Nancy held the cup to my mouth, lowering it when she thought I ought to take a breath, as she had when I was a child. Without asking me, she poured some more, and this time she let me drink it myself. Then she took out the old square biscuit tin, and

172

put it in front of me. After a moment my hand stole out and took a biscuit. 'That's my girlie,' she said.

She asked me no questions. She simply sat down, with her hands folded, and waited. It was peaceful in the kitchen, and safe, and I had no desire to move. I looked at the pale yellow walls, and the dresser with the cups hanging from hooks, and the piles of the *Cork Examiner*, and her knitting bag on the back of the chair. I looked at the television, which my mother had bought her one Christmas, and the old-fashioned wireless, which she refused to replace. The scullery, which contained all the machinery of our lives, the agencies by which we were fed and kept clean, was a place I hardly ever visited, although I sometimes sat with Nancy in her kitchen. On those occasions, as now, we rarely spoke, but I think she liked to have me there.

I had not been there for a long time. Tentatively, I reached out and felt the soft clean surface of her deal table. In the centre stood a blue china fruit bowl, and among the apples and the tangerines there was a packet of the harsh mints that she loved so well. There was always a faint smell of peppermint surrounding her. Then I noticed an enormous and elaborate box of chocolates, and I smiled involuntarily. 'Sydney?' I asked. She nodded. 'Came the minute you left,' she said. 'He was so sorry to miss you. Always comes at Christmas, Mr Goldsmith. I made him a nice little tea, although he didn't want to eat it. Said he was going out to dinner. But I know him. He was going back on the train, back to an empty house, I expect. I gave him a nice boiled egg, and some toast, and some of my fruit cake, and I made him a few sandwiches to take back with him. He sent you his love, Miss Fan. He was sorry to miss you.'

Sydney Goldsmith, in his gangster's overcoat. His unfailing, his discreet fidelity. I had almost forgotten him, yet now I saw him clearly, head cocked, soft brown

173

hat in one hand. I saw him lean over to kiss my mother's forehead, and I heard him say, 'Any time, Beatrice. Call on me any time. My time is yours.' How long ago it seemed that I had stood with Nancy at the door to wave him goodbye. And I never got in touch with him, although he would have been glad of it. He was always fond of me.

Nancy got up and left the room, and after a time I heard bath water running. My coat had steamed and then turned stiff in its creases, and I shrugged out of it. My shoes were muddy and so were my legs; my grey dress, which I should never wear again, seemed to hang on my insignificant body. So great was my fatigue that if I had a conscious wish, it was to remain where I was. I felt old, unwieldy. Slowly, and with great care, I sat up and leaned forward. I doubted whether I was up to the exertion of taking a bath. In the heat which now enveloped me, I could smell the scent which I had put on earlier that evening. It was only my desire to remove it that made me get up and follow Nancy into the bath-room.

She had put out a clean towel for me and a clean nightgown. She had unwrapped a new cake of green soap and put the bathmat on the floor. She waited while I took off my discredited and dirty clothes, and then went away with them. What she did with them I do not know. I never saw them again after that night.

I lay in the water, the kindest of all the elements, the one that welcomes and soothes and cradles you and from which it is difficult to break free. I floated, without thought or memory, only aware that something had happened. That was what my mind kept saying: something has happened. The details escaped me, although I knew that they were all stored somewhere, and could, at some future date, be retrieved, intact. It would be my wearisome task to retrieve them with gusto, to make my

174

readers smile wryly at the accuracy of my detail. No mercy given, none received. And the purpose of it all distinctly questionable. Perhaps to lighten the burden of things left unsaid. For those who put pen to paper do so because they rarely trust their own voices, and, indeed, in society, have very little to say. They are, as I now knew, the least entertaining of guests.

I looked at myself in the long glass, wiping the steam away with the corner of the towel. I saw a slight and almost childish person, with fixed and fearful eyes. Briefly, I even smiled. I congratulated myself on never looking like this when anyone was near; normally, I know, I look rather disdainful. When I was younger, my Aunt Julia had once taken me on one side and told me that I would make myself unpopular unless I took that expression off my face. I had done so then, but lately, very lately, I had found it useful again.

I put on the nightgown, a white nightgown with long sleeves that I did not immediately recognize. This puzzled me, for I am rather particular about my clothes. This, as far as I could judge, had never been worn, for it had long vertical creases in it and smelt of new cotton. It was a pretty garment, with a round neck, and fullness falling from a yoke. I looked rather well in it. But its strangeness puzzled me, and I found myself standing in the middle of the bathroom, wondering where Nancy had found it. Then it came to me. It was one of the nightgowns I had bought for my mother. She had said, 'Far too pretty for me, my darling. You wear it.' And she had smiled, and folded it up again. But I was rather hurt, although I had not shown it, and I had taken it into her room and put it into the drawer of the dressing table with the glass top and all the photographs stuck underneath it. Nancy, of course, had kept it, as she had kept everything else.

Suddenly I wanted to sleep, and I stumbled to the

door and out into the passage. Nancy emerged from the kitchen, and said, 'No dressing gown, Miss Fan? What can you be thinking of?' But I must have looked exhausted, for she took my arm again and guided me. When we reached my door, I made as if to kiss her goodnight, but she said, 'No, dear, no', and went on walking, urging me forward with her. I said, 'What is it? What's the matter?' She went ahead of me, her step more purposeful now. 'Nancy,' I called after her, 'what is it?' Then she turned, her expression guileless. 'You said you wanted a change,' she said, 'so I've put you in Madam's room. Such a nice room. I've made up the bed.'

So I got into that bed, which seemed very strange after my own. And I looked at the ivory satin curtains, and the white rug in front of the pale tiled fireplace, all rather faded now, but made of such superior materials that they would last for ever. And the idiosyncratic centre light, of wrought iron, sprouting many tiny satin shades, that I begged my mother to allow me to change, but she never would. She always wanted everything to stay the same. And although I had not been in this room for a long time, I had no doubt that her clothes were still hanging in the wardrobe, and her narrow shoes marshalled in their usual impeccable rows.

I did not now want to sleep, but I could feel Nancy's hand stroking my own, smoothing it out as it lay on the sheet. Then I felt her hand on my forehead, testing it. And then I felt it across my eyes, as I had so often felt it as a child: the signal to close them. I heard her moving round the room, pulling curtains closer together, touching things on the dressing table. Then I heard her close the door, very quietly, as if I were already asleep.

T W E L V E

I remember that I slept and woke all through the rest of
that short night and that it somehow seemed extremely
long. When Nancy had left the room I got up and pulled
the curtains back and saw that the sky was a dull plum
colour, as it is always supposed to be above an unsleep-
ing city. This was strange, because when I had been out
in it I had been aware only of blackness. Several times
I awoke to see that same uneasy and menacing light,
which seemed to darken and harden as the hours wore
on, falling back into a neutral pallor only before dawn.

Each time I awoke I felt a child's innocence and anticipation, and I would stretch my legs and arms with
pleasure until I remembered where I was and how I
came there. My unconsciousness must have been of a
very strange kind. From black and undisturbed sleep I
would surface every so often – perhaps after only fifteen
minutes or so – into this state of total regression, as if I
were on holiday, being cared for, with a day full of
surprises and treats ahead of me. I think this is one of the
cruellest tricks we play on ourselves, this inability to
banish early expectation. This childlike layer of my
being had apparently been preserved intact, under

177

layers of experience which had settled on it like volcanic ash, and which were dispersed by the action of waking, that immense upward thrust into the light, only to settle again once the superhuman effort had been made. And each time, for a second, I felt the same size, small and spindly, and I could swear there was a smile on my face, the smile of the child who knows that its nurse will soon come to prepare it for the day ahead.

The smile faded rapidly, and with it all hope, but I was not ready to disentangle my situation, and I simply turned over on my side and willed myself to sleep again. The quality of this sleep was dense, thick, engulfing, and I found myself hungry for it, as for some gross food. At one point I could even see my face, eyes tightly shut, mouth full, questing, in my pig-like search for unknowingness. Oddly enough, both the periods of sleep and the mistaken innocence of the awakening were not unpleasant. And the fact that they were so regularly interspersed, and with such frequency, gave me the impression that I was not only being rested but also programmed for the task that lay ahead of me.

I awoke finally and regretfully at about eight o'clock. It was a dull, dark morning, and owing to the position of my mother's bedroom I could hear none of the familiar noises of the street. Instead I heard Nancy shuffling along the passage and I heard the front door open and close behind her. I sat up in the bed and felt those arms and legs, which had been weightless during the night, resume their fatigue and their stiffness. The joints of my feet hurt, and my wrists, when I stretched them out in front of me, seemed thinner. I had thought, during some brief practical moments, that I might spend the morning in bed, for there was no work to do, nothing to get up for. The presents were all wrapped. I had helped Nancy with the shopping at the weekend. I had nothing to do. But in fact I was anxious to get up. I felt a curious distaste for my unclothed self, as if my naked state were an offence. For this reason, when I drew off the night-gown the sight of my body filled me with shame, so lacking did I perceive it to be in adult qualities, so flat, so unremarkable, so humiliated. I wondered if this feeling would ever leave me or whether I was condemned to see myself in this manner for the rest of my life.

I bathed again, and dressed very carefully. I put on cheerful clothes, my blue woollen shirt and my blue pullover. I paid great attention to my appearance and even to my well-being. I made no objections when Nancy insisted on my eating two boiled eggs for breakfast, and I sat unprotesting at the kitchen table while she fussed around me. I ate some toast and drank two cups of tea, chewing very carefully, as if I must now get into some sort of training, husbanding my physical energy for the task ahead. Nancy was very pleased with my appetite and scolded me for having got so thin. I had not noticed it until this morning, but now that she mentioned it I could feel the angular bones of my shoulders and my skirt was slightly loose around my waist. I did not mind. It seemed to me appropriate that I should dwindle, that I should shed my biological characteristics. In future I would become subsumed into my head, and into my hand, my writing hand.

The problem was how to fill the rest of the day, for when I had made my bed and tidied the room it was still only half-past nine. I thought I might begin writing straight away, but I found myself sitting in my mother's chair, my hands quite idle, while the day, lightless and dreary, unfolded without me. Far from being the poised satirist of my fantasy and my intention, I found myself returned to my childhood, to those empty winter afternoons when I had to sit quietly because my mother was resting. I missed the Library and saw what life would be like if I had no work to go to. But then I reminded myself that I carried my work about with me, and with a great effort I got up and found a notebook and a pen and sat down again to make notes for my novel, the characters of which were so very real to me and so near. Yet when Nancy called me for lunch I was still sitting there, in the same chair, and I had written nothing of consequence.

Nancy had cooked fish and the smell hung about in the passage, thick and dull and penetrating. I felt it in the curtains, I felt it in my hair, and the inside of my mouth felt dry with it. She must have noticed my peculiar state – which was in fact a suspension of all normal states – and she asked me if I was all right. 'Oh, of course,' I said. 'Not going to work always takes a bit of getting used to. I think it's almost more tiring staying at home', and as I said this I stifled a yawn. But she was quick to see this, and also the fact that I could not finish my food. 'You'd best have a rest,' she remarked. 'You'd best get into bed for an hour. You can take a book in with you,' she added. As if I were very young.

And so, with a feeling of inevitability, I took off my clothes again, and got into bed, not expecting to sleep or even desiring to, but rather taking up the requisite position for reflection or for self-communion. I sat up in the bed, as if marooned on a great raft, and I must have stayed there, quite unmoving, for over an hour. Despite my excellent intentions I could not escape a mood of lethargy that was almost one of mourning. What disturbed me most was my absence of anger, for without anger where is the satire? I felt instead a weariness, and an understanding that extended even to my companions of the night before. I felt in my bones, and this may merely have been extreme fatigue (but I doubt it), that those people were innocent of everything except greed, that, like children or animals, they simply took what they wanted. That this was the law. In the light of my sad day, I saw their faces again, sly, flushed, their eyes sliding sideways, as if to see if anyone were catching them out ... Eating too much, filling their smeared mouths with sweetness. Having a party, a celebration. Laughing too loudly, dressing up. I saw that they were children, much as I had been in my sleep, or in my waking moments, and that they would inevitably, at some point, feel that momentary desolation that afflicts the grown child, the child without parents, elders. That they would start, and look puzzled, look annoyed, and their annoyance would fade into bewilderment. And then all their haughty ways would be of as little use to them as my sharp tongue was to me. The only difference was that they would comfort each other, for they were good at crying out objections and complaints. Whereas I would simply be here, not knowing how to recover, but working at it, with my pen and my notebook.

I could not even side against them. I was not of their number, that was all. The moment at which I recognized this difference was the ultimate sadness, and I felt all my assumed certainties dropping away from me as if they had been fashionable clothes which I had perhaps tried on in a shop and then regretfully laid aside, as being ... not suitable. I thought with longing and even with affection of the times we had spent together, the laughter, which had been genuine, the enormous fascination of their selfish hedonism, the curious attention I had brought to the business of watching them. I thought, first, and instinctively, of Nick and Alix, and I remembered how they had delivered me from various prospective prisons – old age, silence, solitude – and how I had risen at their command as if I had been waiting for it all my life. I remembered how they had introduced me to the true, the saving selfishness, and how, under their tuition, I had distanced myself from sad people to whom I could bring no joy, nothing but my presence and my helpless company. I thought of the evenings, and how I had swung across the park, confident of the entertainment I should find at the end of my journey. I thought of the day we had motored out to Bray, and I remembered the photograph: I remembered the sound of the last leaves falling silently on the lawn as we sat in the mellow sun, in almost unexpected warmth, and how only the slight coldness stealing up from the river let us know that this was winter and not spring.

I remembered, as one does, how the weather was always better then, colours more vivid, appetite sharper, energy unending. I looked back, as if from a great distance, at that autumn and the notable benefits it had brought me, and I saw myself, in my rather nice cream suit, walking down Sloane Street: I thought, as I saw myself, how eager and elegant I looked. And this brought me back to my present situation, lying in bed at two o'clock in the afternoon, thin, watchful, neither very young nor very old, but in fact a mind destined to grow older in a body destined to appear ever more childish. The bonhomie of those autumn days had freeze-dried into endless wariness.

And yet even then I hoped that I might see them again. I missed them too much, and the lessons that they taught, to forego them altogether. I needed their company, their enjoyment, even if I was not of their number. I needed to study them, I needed them for material. And if I ever found the courage for a last throw of the dice, I needed to take them on again. I needed to watch them at Christmas; I needed to see their grasping hands, their infallible appetites; I needed their profligacy, on which I could always depend. I needed their gusto, so appropriate to the Christmas season, when eyes glisten with covetousness and excess, when appetites expand and are never sated, when affection is extended to the watchers at the feast. I wanted, quite simply, to spend

Christmas with those lords of misrule, in heat and noise, amid platefuls of sucked bones and the collapsing ruins of puddings, at a table awash with glossy leaves and discarded wrappings, the air blue with the smoke from monster cigars, and idle hands searching lazily for nuts, sweetmeats, marzipan. No sacramental Christmas, this. But how much more desirable than my blameless household, with its smell of dead fish, its muffled dusty heat, its untouched furniture, and the shuffle of slippered feet outside my door.

If I thought of James, and I tried not to, it was with a feeling of dread, for I now realized that he was accessible to others but not to me. What I had witnessed had made it impossible for me to think that evidence out of the way. For once a thing is known, it can never be unknown. It can only be forgotten. And in the unlikely event of my forgetting, he would not forget, or rather, he would be aware of a small danger signal somewhere in his consciousness which would remind him of my watching eye and my writing hand, and he would stay away from me. It seemed to me that I, rather than he, had brought this about, and my despair was extreme. For now that I knew that I loved him, it was his whole life that I loved. And I would never know that life. Changes would no doubt take place, and I would not even know what they were. 'How is he?' I would long to ask. But there would be no one to ask. If I were to pass him in the corridor, or in the Library, I would have to smile like the stranger he wanted me to be. And if I wished to please him, I must simply stay away. And his life, his life ... would go on without me. And I would have no knowledge of it. And since I had apparently understood so little, I could not even blame him. I get things wrong, you see.

This conclusion moved me to restlessness, and again I wondered if the position could not be retrieved. I thought with terror of the days and nights ahead of me, of the months and the years in which nothing might change and I might become as old and discreet as Nancy. And I think I then resolved to find the courage to fight this fate, and to ring up and let them know that I was fine, that I was looking forward to seeing them. On their terms, let it be understood. There would be no need to spell this out; the message would be quite clear. And if I were very careful, and husbanded my looks and my expressions of doubt or blame, perhaps they would allow me back. Of course, my status would be changed. I would be humbler, more subordinate. That was the price to be paid. And I would pay it. But if, at the same time, I were to make notes for a satirical novel...? If they were to meet their fate at my hands, and all un-knowing, would this not be a very logical development?

The idea excited me and put an end to my musings. Already I could feel that chemical sharpness beginning to take command, and I switched off that inward eye, which is called, erroneously, in my opinion, the bliss of solitude, and switched on the outer one, focusing once again on the white wardrobes with sliding doors, the edges of which were picked out in gold, the oyster satin curtains, the fluffy white bedside rugs, the pink quartz elephant bookends, the pink opaline bowl of pot pourri on the dressing table, the silver-backed brushes, and the small cut-glass tray with its pink velvet pin cushion and ivory-handled manicure set. I believe this stuff is worth quite a bit these days; I must get an estimate some time. I swung my legs out of the bed and rushed into my clothes, the cheerful blue shirt and pullover, the blue wool skirt. I sat down at the dressing table and brushed my hair, and as I looked into the glass I congratulated myself on my steadiness. I saw no ghosts. And beyond my reflection in the glass I caught sight of a framed, tinted engraving hanging on the opposite wall. This

184

showed an eighteenth-century scene of skaters, doll-like figures with muffs and wide skirts or tricorne hats and tight-fitting satin breeches. I had always loved it as a child, but I could not then read what was written underneath. The words now seemed to me singularly apposite. They read, '*Glissez, mortels; n'appuyez pas.*' Alluding to the thinness of the ice, of course. This seemed to me a good omen, and I resolved to behave in a suitably light and elegant manner.

I was hungry now, and thirsty, the motor of my appetite running again. I stood up and reviewed myself, and saw the mask of amusement back in place, my physical being neat and collected, and poised for action. I made the bed, and opened the window, and went over to the engraving, and gave it an approving tap. The doll-like faces, preserved in an eternal youthfulness, totally devoid of expression or emotion, stared back at me, reminding me that I too was young, and not without resource. I shut the door behind me and made for the kitchen, in search of tea.

I found Nancy fussing over a multiplicity of tins – round tins, square tins, polygonal tins – and removing from them various cakes and biscuits. She makes these all the time but I have no idea who eats them. I think she likes sweet things, and, as most old people will, she prefers to nibble at something light rather than to eat a proper meal. The room was very warm, and I noticed that she had also made about two dozen mince pies. The beautiful smell hung in the air, and as they cooled on a wire tray I could see the enticing gleam where the mincemeat had oozed through the pastry. I have to say that she is not a very good cook, and her cakes are normally rather heavy; in addition, they are stuffed so full of fruit that they last for ever. I cannot imagine what becomes of them in the end. One of the attractions of James (yes, I managed to think of him quite calmly) was

185

that he always ate up the buns and biscuits she left out on the tray for us. This, of course, merely incited her to bake more.

She seemed to be arranging some sort of party, and when I asked her if she was expecting someone, she said, 'I dare say Mr Reardon will look in.' Of course, I am never at home in the afternoon and it did not occur to me that Nancy was off-loading all her baking on to Mr Reardon, who apparently still came up with the evening paper, before going round to the betting shop to collect his winnings. I had thought of having a quick cup of tea and going back to write a bit, but this was quite opportune, for the Christmas civilities had to be exchanged at some point, and I might as well get them over as soon as possible.

Mr Reardon was obviously a keen cake man, for I counted four varieties on the table, all rather hefty. The bell rang just as Nancy was pouring the tea, and as I went to answer the door I found myself hoping that this could be got over fairly quickly. Mr Reardon is a charming man and has been in this building for as long as I can remember. He is very small and quiet and corpulent, and I think he suffers from high blood pressure. He wears a sort of blue uniform, which obviously dates from earlier days, for it is now much too tight for him; it seems to compress his short body and drive the blood to his head, for he moves his neck round with caution, and his small gooseberry-coloured eyes seem quite suffused with the effort to stay open. He is long past retiring age, and he stays on because he likes the work and takes a pride in the building and its tenants; the management, of course, are delighted.

Mr Reardon, perhaps because of his age and his blood pressure, cannot tackle all the heavy jobs, such as the heaving about of dustbins, and for this he has an assistant, an aberrant youth whom my father used to refer to as the boy, although he is now much older and is to be addressed as Mr Fentiman. There is something wrong with him too, but I think that Mr Reardon has him under control. Mr Fentiman talks to himself in a menacing manner and sometimes makes threatening gestures with his arm. His appearance does not inspire much confidence, for he wears a cap planted rather low on his forehead and a donkey jacket with the collar perpetually turned up, so that his face appears to be watching from behind a gun emplacement. He shaves once a week and has a cigarette planted in his mouth; he never removes the cigarette, and should you speak to him while he is coughing, you will receive the full brunt of the ash.

I saw, with sinking heart, that Mr Reardon had brought Mr Fentiman with him, cigarette and all, and I prepared myself to weather a tea party. Nancy was delighted, and once we were all seated it was clear to me that this went on every afternoon, and that in fact it was I who was intruding. But they were extremely nice to me, and urged me to eat, and as I sat, playing with a few crumbs, I watched in fascination as Mr Reardon filled and emptied his plate and drank cup after cup of tea, to Nancy's beaming approval. Mr Fentiman, his cap firmly in place, attempted at one point to relate a fairly incoherent story about an intruder he had discovered lurking in one of the garages, but, 'That'll do, Arthur,' said Mr Reardon, accepting his third cup of tea, and running a finger round his collar, 'no need to upset the ladies.' He then asked our permission to smoke, and when I went to get an ash-tray (the green malachite one with the cockatoo on the rim) I took the opportunity to pick up their two envelopes from the desk, and I put these beside their plates when I went back. Mr Fentiman's plate, of course, was already full of ash.

'Very kind of you, miss,' said Mr Reardon, and made

a sign to Mr Fentiman who bounded off and within a minute bounded back again, with a wrapped bottle in his hand. 'I took the liberty', Mr Reardon went on, 'of bringing a small token for Miss Mulvaney, who has been so very kind with her hospitality. I have been very happy here,' he said, simply, and handed Nancy the bottle. 'You shouldn't have,' said Nancy, who is always confused when people give her things and who always protests, but I made her unwrap it, and, since it was clear that this must be accorded its due solemnity, I fetched four glasses. 'I'll give you a toast,' said Mr Reardon, raising his glass of cherry brandy. 'On your feet, Arthur. Good will to all men,' and he emptied his glass. 'Hear, hear,' I said, since something was called for, and managed to swallow a mouthful of the cherry brandy, which was disconcertingly thick and icy. 'I'll have mine later,' said Nancy, who always used to say this when my father poured her a glass of sherry before lunch on Sunday; she was always torn between the horror of drinking it and the fear of hurting him. I could see that the same conflict was raging now. 'You'll like it, Nan,' I urged her. 'It's sweet', but, 'I'll have it with my supper,' she assured us, and put it behind her on the dresser.

Mr Reardon was now disposed to reminisce, which I dreaded. He always had a few words to say about my father, whom he had greatly admired, and of course he had been very fond of my mother. I remember him wiping a tear from those small gooseberry eyes when he came up to enquire about her, as he always did, and I had to tell him it was too late ... His small fat fingers, slightly stained with nicotine, shakily unfolding a handkerchief with a striped border ... In order to forestall this, I asked him where he was spending Christmas, and was told that he was going to his married daughter in Harrow. 'But I shall be back in the evening,' he assured us. 'I won't leave you ladies alone all day. Most people are away, of course. Mrs Hunt went yesterday. Even Lady Cohen has gone, although with her leg I doubt if it's wise.' We all nodded, ruminative, in the kitchen grown warm and hazy with smoke.

Out of the corner of my eye I could see that the time was creeping on towards five o'clock, and I began to urge them, silently, to leave. Finally I stood up, and said, 'You must excuse me. I have some writing to do. But please stay, both of you.' The men stood up, with a scraping of chairs. 'Happy Christmas, miss,' said Mr Reardon. 'I know you miss your dear ones. Only natural. Door, Arthur,' he rapped out, as I seemed determined to escape. 'But their memories are safe in our hearts,' he went on, the cherry brandy evidently having gone to his head, and memories of Armistice Day floating unbidden into his mind. 'We shall not forget.' 'Hear, hear,' echoed Mr Fentiman.

At the door I turned and saw them, all standing gravely behind the table, looking at me, their faces deeply shadowed by the harsh centre light. The table was still strewn with sticky glasses and the crumbs of all the cakes, and these childish attributes seemed ill-suited to their bleak faces. Nancy and Mr Reardon seemed to be posing for a last photograph, their stubby hands placed on the table in front of them. Mr Fentiman, behind his upturned collar and his cigarette, looked, although dangerous, a survivor, not of starvation or political wrongs, but of who knew what deprivations of a more domestic kind. It was clear from their expressions that they were concerned for me. That although I was, from their point of view, one of the advantaged, they nevertheless regarded me as being at risk.

As I closed the door behind me, I felt as if I were shutting myself out of light and comfort. I went into the drawing room and switched on the lamps and the fire, but it seemed inappropriate for me to be there on my own, and I disliked the social distinction it seemed to raise between those people and myself. After wandering round rather restlessly for a few moments, I switched everything off again and went back to my mother's bedroom. It felt quite natural for me to be there, although I postponed the removal of my clothes from my own room to hers: that was a task for which I was not prepared. Perhaps Nancy could do it for me, I thought, with a slight falling away of my earlier confidence. I sat down in the pink velvet chair, and it came to me, for the first time that day, that I might be alone at Christmas. This, in its turn, brought back the worrying thoughts that had pursued me earlier, and, almost as if for protection, I got up and found my notebook and my pen, and sat down again, determined to write something.

And I did. I made notes for my novel, and I found that it was going very well and very fast, that the characters emerged quite naturally, and that, quite naturally, I found the right words with which to describe them. The words, in fact, which had previously deserted me, were fairly pouring out. The fact that I was skating over the surface, jazzing things up, playing for laughs, may have had something to do with it. I laughed myself, at one point. It was quite easy, really. I managed to kill a couple of hours in this manner. I did not even hear Nancy's guests leave.

Then, I don't quite know why, I stopped. It was as if my little fund of amusement was exhausted, and even the knowledge that I could manage this if I wanted to, and that I had found a suitable occupation for myself in the days, the months ahead, did not concern me. I got up and walked to the window, and could see nothing but my own self, reflected in the black glass. I thought of my lost hopes, and how lucky I was to be able to convert them so easily into satire. Now the holiday would pass almost unnoticed, because I should be absorbed in my

190

task. And how, probably before the New Year (only a week away), I should ring up the Frasers, with my good wishes, and say, 'Oh, by the way, I'm writing that novel I was always talking about. It's taking up all my time. But do let's have dinner one evening. It's been such ages. And if you see James, do wish him a Happy New Year for me.' A face-saving operation. And also an investment. For I must go back to them and study them anew; I must know them once again at first hand.

Yet, moving restlessly about the room, I found myself saying, 'This will not do.' Something was false, out of alignment, not giving a true note. And, in almost physical distress, I moved my head from side to side, wondering what was wrong. And then I became quiet, for I realized that I was still waiting, hoping that one of them would telephone and invite me to their Christmas celebration.

Of course, this might not happen. For once a thing is known, it can never be unknown. It can only be forgotten. And, in a way that bends time, once it is remembered, it indicates the future. I realize now that although I sit in this room, growing older, alone, and very sadly, I must live by that knowledge. The telephone may ring, tonight or tomorrow: it no longer matters. Someone may spare me a thought, probably Alix, who was always very kind. 'Hey, hey,' she will say, 'is that Little Orphan Fanny?' And, at the very last moment, I shall be invited to their Christmas celebration. I have no idea whether I shall go or not. In a sense, it makes no difference, for the matter is already prejudged, marked off. It has already been lived through. It has existed.

After that last sentence, I moved to the bed and switched on the bedside lamp. With the letting down of this final barrier between myself and the truth I seemed to welcome back those images which used to throng my mind. The window, black with night, shuts me in, and

I see in its reflection Dr Constantine, crouched over the telephone, his brown eye vacant and without resource. I see Dr Simek braced against the back of his chair, his amber cigarette holder clenched in his teeth. I see Mrs Halloran, becalmed on her bed in South Kensington, a bottle beside her. I see Miss Morpeth, writing to her niece. I see myself.

Nancy shuffles down the passage, and I hear her locking the front door. It is very quiet now. A voice says, 'My darling Fan.' I pick up my pen. I start writing.